Book Six

EPIC ZERO 6

Tales of a Major Meta Disaster

By

R.L. Ullman

But That's
Another Story...
Press

Cover design by Yusup Mediyan
All character images created with heromachine.com.

Published by But That's Another Story... Press
Ridgefield, CT

4.202/

Printed in the United States of America.

First Printing, 2019.

ISBN: 978-0-9984129-8-6
Library of Congress Control Number: 2019914345

For Matthew,
my Meta 4

TABLE OF CONTENTS

ONE

I CAN'T DO ANYTHING RIGHT

For some reason, I don't have a good feeling about this.

Maybe it's because we're orbiting two hundred miles above Earth on a blacked-out International Space Station. Or maybe it's because there's no sign of the crew, whose last transmission was Code Red, which basically means 'extreme danger.' Or maybe it's because the Meta Monitor picked up a mysterious Meta 3 signature coming from the space station it could only classify as: *Identity Unknown*.

So, yeah, I don't have a good feeling about this.

In fact, I'm pretty darn creeped out.

Fortunately, we have our flashlights so we can see, but the constant BUZZING from the emergency alarm isn't doing much to calm my nerves either. Plus, unlike the Waystation where we have the benefit of TechnocRat's Gravitational Stabilizer, the International Space Station doesn't have artificial gravity. So that means we're floating around like weightless balloons.

Just. Freaking. Wonderful.

Unfortunately, the crummy conditions aren't even the worst part. Not by a longshot. The worst part is that the team decided to put *me* in charge of this rescue mission!

"Me?" I said when they told me. "Why me?"

"Because it's part of your development," Dad said. "Learning how to manage a team in dangerous situations is an important part of being a leader. We've been training your sister, and now it's your turn."

"I see," I said. "But you realize I'm just a kid, right?"

Well, clearly Dad didn't care about that, because here I am, 'leading' Dad and Shadow Hawk—two of the greatest Meta heroes of all time—on this spooky mission.

"What next fearless leader?"

Oh, and Grace, my lovely sister, is here too.

I shine my flashlight on her frowning face.

"Relax," I say. "I've got this."

But honestly, I've pretty much got nothing. I mean, we still have no idea what happened to the astronauts on board, and the Meta Monitor didn't provide much help either. But I do know one thing, I can't fail, because if I do Grace will never let me hear the end of it.

So, that leaves only one option.

Don't screw it up.

There are two exits out of the docking port, left or right. Now, which way should we go? I do a quick round of eeny meeny miny moe—my favorite decision-making tool—and land on left. But as soon as I grab a handhold and poke my head through the airlock, I'm blinded by a flashing light from above.

I stagger backward disoriented. It takes a few seconds to stop seeing stars, but when I do, I find myself staring at Grace's charming face.

"You're such a goober," she says, rolling her eyes.

"Are you hurt, kid?" Shadow Hawk asks.

"Nope," I say. "Just my pride."

I curse under my breath. If I'm going to lead this team to find the missing crew members, I can't make rookie mistakes like that again. I have to do better.

"Follow me," I say. "Oh, and don't look up."

This time I shield my eyes as I float through the airlock into a cargo hold filled with crates tied down by ropes. As I drift past, I read a few of the labels: *Dry Goods, Backup Robot Crane, Extravehicular Mobility Units.* Nothing seems out of the ordinary, but there's still no sign of the crew.

I push through to the next room and scan with my flashlight. It's a small room with a long table bolted to the floor and a pole holding a bunch of I.V. pouches. Okay, I'm clearly in the medical wing. But it's empty.

Then, I notice something floating by my face.

I shine my flashlight and scream in horror!

"What?" Dad asks, floating in. "What is it?"

"It's a... a...," I mutter, completely breathless.

"It's a glove," Grace says matter-of-factly, snatching it out of the air. "It looks like an astronaut's glove." Then, she looks at me with a smirk. "Wait, did you think it was, like, an actual hand or something?"

"Um, no," I say, lying through my teeth.

"Holy cow," she says. "Who put this guy in charge?"

Thank goodness it's pitch black in here, otherwise, they'd see I'm red with embarrassment. Honestly, I don't know why I'm so jittery. I mean, I've handled far worse situations than this. I've got to calm down.

"Follow me," I say, trying to sound confident.

"I'm afraid to," Grace remarks.

I ignore her and duck through the next portal, entering into a large chamber filled with scientific equipment. This must be the laboratory. Part of the crew's mission is to conduct research experiments, so everything here looks normal. I even recognize a few things I've seen in TechnocRat's lab, like an incubator and a centrifuge.

But then, I notice something odd.

In the center of the room is a metal table with four straps lying across its surface. Strangely, the straps are fastened, but they aren't holding anything down. It's only when I take a step closer that I see a big, uneven hole in the middle of the table like something chewed its way through the metal itself.

I kneel to look beneath the table when my flashlight catches a strand of something long and translucent. It looks like... a spider web? Except, it's purple. And as I bend over, I see even more webbing stretched across the legs of the table.

I poke it with my finger. It's taut and sticky, just like a spider web, but a whole lot thicker.

Did I mention that I hate spiders?

Then, I remember something. I didn't see spiders on the space station's inventory list. I guess it could be a stowaway. But why would its web be purple? Unless...

A chill runs down my spine.

"We're in the research lab," I say.

"Yeah, Captain Obvious," Grace says. "So?"

"So," I say, pointing my light down at the webbing. "Do you know any spiders that spin purple webs?"

"No," Grace says, kneeling to look.

"Or eats through metal?" I add, pointing to the table.

"Nope," she says.

"Exactly," I say. "I think we found the source of the problem. I bet the crew caught something they shouldn't have and brought it on board. Something alien."

"What?" Grace says. "Are you serious?"

"Dead serious," I say.

Who knows? Maybe I'm wrong. But when I turn to get Dad's opinion, I realize Grace and I are all alone.

"Hey, where are the other guys?" I ask.

"What?" Grace says, turning around. "They were right behind me a second ago."

"Captain Justice?" I call out, pushing myself back to the entrance. "Shadow Hawk? Where are you guys?"

I shine my flashlight all around but I don't see them.

"I can't believe it," I say, turning back to Grace. "It's like they vanished without a—"

But suddenly, I'm talking to no one.

Because Grace is gone as well.

"Glory Girl?" I call out, my voice echoing through the chamber. Where'd she go? I shine my flashlight all around. "Okay, guys, this game of hide-and-seek isn't funny. Come out, come out, wherever you are."

But no one shows up.

Suddenly, my skin feels all goose-pimply.

I'm alone.

But the problem is, I'm not alone, because whatever nabbed them is probably watching me right now!

Then, something catches my eye.

On the far side of the chamber is a light. That's funny, I don't remember seeing a light there before, but it's clearly there now. And a door is cracked open!

Okay, I've got two choices. Either I can leave now and get reinforcements, or I can press on and see what's behind door number one. I swallow hard.

Why did I have to be the leader?

I float carefully towards the door and grab a

handhold to steady myself. Then, I hang there, pressing my ear against the door. But I don't hear anything. Now what?

I mean, I've got no clue what's happening on the other side, but I'm pretty sure it's bad news. And even though every bone in my body wants to flee, I can't just leave my team behind. What's that old saying—the captain always goes down with the ship?

I take a deep breath and exhale. Okay, here goes nothing. I grab the door handle, pull it open, and float inside. Immediately, I see a giant windshield, a navigation control station, and a captain's chair and I know I've reached the command center.

But then I do a double take because stretched across the twenty-foot windshield is a gigantic purple web—and stuck to it are three large objects wrapped head-to-toe in purple webbing!

At first, my mind tells me there must be some really massive flies on this ship. But then I realize one of the flies is much smaller than the others, and it hits me.

Those aren't flies at all.

That's Dad, Shadow Hawk, and Grace!

If I don't get them out of there, they'll suffocate!

I reach into my utility belt for something sharp, when I notice a large shadow expanding beneath my feet.

I freeze, petrified by what could be hovering overhead. And when I look up, I'm not disappointed, because lowering itself from the ceiling is a grizzly, refrigerator-sized spider-creature with multiple eyes, purple hair, and a gaggle of spindly legs all ending in razor-sharp tips.

Did I mention that I hate alien spiders?

"Oh, sorry," I say, trying to keep from passing out. "Didn't mean to bug you."

But it just narrows its eyes and keeps on coming.

"Not a talker, huh?" I say. "Well, how about you relax and stream the latest Spider-Man reboot off the web while I free my friends here?"

But instead of laughing, the creature swings its front leg! I barely duck out of the way before it slices a monitor clean in two.

Well, now I know where to go for my next haircut. But I still have no clue what its Meta powers are. Unless looking creepy is a new kind of Meta classification.

I've got to keep it off balance. But when I open my mouth to offer yet another witty barb, no sound comes out. Huh? That's weird. I try talking again, but I can't hear my own voice. What's going on?

But it looks like I won't have time to figure it out because the beast floats to the ground and I realize I'm in for the gravity-defying fight of my life!

Then, its long legs hit the tile, and it launches at me!

I push hard off the nearest computer terminal and drift away, bumping into the wall behind me. But strangely there's no sound when I make contact.

Huh? What happened to all of the noise?

And then a lightbulb goes off.

Grace, Dad, and Shadow Hawk didn't make a peep when they were captured. And now I can't even hear myself talk. I connect the dots and realize this thing must have the power to squash sound!

Well, that's clever. I bet it uses its power to mute the cries of its victims. That's perfect for a predator like him.

But the thing is, I've got powers too.

I concentrate hard, duplicating Dad's Super-Strength. And none too soon, because seconds later, the spider attacks! I sideswipe a barrage of slowly swinging legs and counter with a slow-motion roundhouse kick of my own, sending the creature drifting into a wall of computers.

Not bad.

Who knew I was a zero-gravity Kung Fu master?

But when the creature connects, sparks fly from the computer bank behind it, and the entire station tilts forward and then takes off in reverse!

Oh no! That spider must have crashed into the thruster propulsion control panel!

Luckily, I manage to grab the arm of a chair that's bolted to the floor, but everything not tied down is being thrown towards the windshield!

Fortunately, Dad, Grace, and Shadow Hawk are still stuck to the web, but the spider isn't so lucky. For a second, I chuckle to myself as the creature slowly plummets with everything else. But my glee quickly turns to horror as one of its razor-sharp legs pierces the windshield and a giant crack begins to crisscross the glass pane.

Um, that's not good.

The windshield could—

SHATTER!

Suddenly, an incredible force pulls everything towards the opening—including me! I wrap my arms around the chair as my feet lift off the ground! I've got to hold on! If I get sucked out of here, I'll die in deep space!

Out of the corner of my eye, I see the spider get vacuumed right out of the space station! That's great news, but this isn't exactly how things were supposed to go!

The force is pulling me hard!

I grip tighter, but I can feel my fingers giving way!

Then, I remember I can end this.

I just need to say the words.

I try calling out, but somehow the spider's noise-canceling powers are still in effect! And the creature is too far gone for me to negate its power!

I feel my fingers unraveling…

I'm… going… to…

"GISMO!" comes a female voice. "End program!"

"Training module ended, Ms. Understood," Gismo says.

I hit the floor hard, knocking the wind out of me. And when I roll over, the International Space Station is gone.

I'm back in the Combat Room, and boy am I relieved. I hope the team is okay. OMG! The team!

I pop back up to find Dad, Grace, and Shadow Hawk lying on the floor behind me, catching their breath.

Thank goodness they're alive!

"Elliott Harkness!" Mom says. "What's going on down here?"

"Well," I say, "Dad put me in charge, and—"

"He did, did he?" she says, wheeling on Dad.

"Well," Dad says sheepishly. "We did agree we wanted him to become a better leader."

"Yes," Mom says. "But we didn't agree we'd kill him in the process."

"Hang on," Grace says. "Can I get a vote on that?"

"If I hadn't come looking for you," Mom continues, ignoring Grace, "who knows what could have happened? That was an advanced module. He's not ready for that."

"Well," Dad says, "I guess you're right."

"I'm still here," I say. "I can hear you."

"Sorry, son," Dad says, standing up. "Your mother is right. You've done some great things, but leadership is a completely different skillset. Next time we'll start with a more basic training module."

"Next time?" Grace says. "Next time leave me out of it. He may be powerful, but he ain't no leader."

"Enough, Grace," Mom says.

I want to tell her off, but she's right. I'm a terrible leader. A terrible leader who nearly got everyone killed.

"Thanks for the save," Shadow Hawk says to Mom. "But what *are* you doing here? Is something wrong?"

"Oh no," Mom says, the color draining from her face. "I got totally distracted. We've got to get upstairs. We just received a message from the White House. The president needs to speak with us urgently."

Meta Profile
The Freedom Force

Captain Justice
Class: Super-Strength
Meta: ▪▪▪▫

Ms. Understood
Class: Psychic
Meta: ▪▪▫▫

Glory Girl
Class: Flight
Meta: ▪▪▫

Shadow Hawk
Class: None
Meta:

Epic Zero
Class: Meta Manipulator
Meta: ▪▪▪▪

TechnocRat
Class: Super-Intellect
Meta: ▪▪▪▪

Blue Bolt
Class: Super-Speed
Meta: ▪▪▪▫

Master Mime
Class: Magic
Meta: ▪▪▪▫

Makeshift
Class: Energy Manipulator
Meta: ▪

TWO

I RECEIVE AN EXECUTIVE ORDER

By the time we reach the Mission Room, TechnocRat has the video feed ready to go.

"What took you guys so long?" he asks, typing on a keyboard with his white tail.

"There's no time to explain," Mom says.

"Got it," TechnocRat says, looking at me. "So, what did you do this time?"

"*Me?*" I say. "Nothing."

"Yep," Grace says. "That about sums it up."

"Shut it," I say.

"Make me," Grace says.

"Enough," Mom says. "We're about to speak to the president of the United States. Can the two of you please show some self-control?"

"I can," Grace says, smoothing her cape, "but I'm not so sure about him. By the way, you're not going to let the president see him looking like that, are you?"

"Hey!" I say. "I look fine. Um, don't I?"

"Quiet," Dad says. "Is it on?"

"Yep," TechnocRat says. "We're waiting on them."

"Where's the rest of the team?" Shadow Hawk asks.

"On a mission," TechnocRat says. "But they haven't answered my calls. So, either they're in the middle of a fight or Makeshift lost his communicator again."

"I'd bet on the latter," Grace says.

"Hold on," TechnocRat says. "A signal is coming through. We should have a visual in three… two…"

Suddenly, the monitor flicks on and I stand up a little straighter, excited for my first meeting with the actual president. But when the picture comes in, it's not the president we see, but our friends Blue Bolt, Makeshift, and Master Mime.

"Oh, hey guys," Dad says. "It's great seeing you, but I thought we were talking to the president?"

But the heroes don't answer.

Instead, they just stare at us blankly.

"Um, guys?" Dad says. "Is something wrong?"

But as the camera pans out, I realize something is very wrong, because the heroes are on their knees wearing handcuffs! Except their handcuffs don't look like normal handcuffs, but rather like thick, leather wrappings.

"What's on their wrists?" Grace asks.

But no one can answer her, not even TechnocRat.

Yet, for some reason, that leathery material looks strangely familiar to me.

"What's going on here?" Mom asks.

"They've been captured," Shadow Hawk says.

Suddenly, the camera pulls back even farther and we realize our friends are kneeling on the steps of a super-long, concrete building in front of a large portico. And they're surrounded by a dozen ginormous, armor-plated robots, each painted army green!

"Where are they?" Grace whispers. "And what are those metal bot thingies?"

"They're at the Pentagon," Shadow Hawk answers. "The home of our nation's Department of Defense. But I've never seen those robots before."

"Blue Bolt," Dad says. "Where's the president? Is she safe?"

"Don't worry, Captain Justice," comes a female voice. "I'm right here."

Suddenly, the camera swings left, landing on a steely-eyed woman with gray streaks in her hair. I'd know her face anywhere. It's President Kara Kensington! And standing behind her are a bunch of military officers.

"President Kensington," Dad says. "Are you okay? Do you know what's happened to our colleagues?"

"I appreciate your concern," she says, "but I'm just fine. Your friends, however, aren't feeling so chipper."

"What's going on here?" Dad asks.

"What's going on here is a new direction for America," President Kensington says. "It is my privilege to inform you that Congress just passed a new law called the Meta Restriction Resolution. That means that as of today, all Metas are required to surrender themselves to the government of the United States of America immediately. Therefore, I order you, and all of your Meta friends, to come down to the Pentagon to turn yourselves in at once. The Meta age is officially over."

"What?" Mom says. "Where did this come from?"

But as I scan the crowd behind her, I already know the answer. Because standing to the right of the President is a thin man with piercing blue eyes and a white crewcut—and his name is General William Winch!

The last time I had the displeasure of his company was when I got roped into appearing on the CNC Morning Newsflash to debate the merits of Meta humans. He swore he'd take down all Metas if it was the last thing he ever did.

It looks like he's succeeding.

"President Kensington," Dad says, "is this a joke? The Freedom Force has defended the United States and the world on countless occasions. We've even taken on assignments to protect national security at your request. What you're saying doesn't make sense. And why weren't we notified about this resolution?"

"I'm notifying you now," President Kensington says

firmly. "And I assure you this is no joke. Let me be clear. Our country is run by the will of the people, and the people have decided that Metas are no longer the solution. Metas are the problem."

"But that's ridiculous," Mom says. "What happens when the next intergalactic terror shows up?"

"*If* that happens, Ms. Understood," President Kensington says, "we'll handle it. Just like we've handled your friends here. After all, our new Meta-Buster army is specifically designed to take down Meta threats."

"Interesting," TechnocRat remarks, stroking his whiskers. "I didn't know our government was even capable of developing such sophisticated technology."

"Madame President," Dad says. "We respectfully request that you free our colleagues. They're heroes."

"Really?" she says. "Because our statistics say otherwise. Did you know, Captain, that ninety-seven percent of all crimes are committed by Metas? Or that costs to repair damage from Meta battles have increased over three hundred percent from a year ago? Or that insurance premiums for regular citizens living in Meta-afflicted areas have risen nine thousand percent? America has had enough. The Meta problem stops now."

"Oh, really?" Grace barks. "And what are you planning to do with 'Meta problems' like us who turn themselves in?"

"Glory Girl!" Mom says.

"Hold on," Shadow Hawk says. "That's an excellent

question."

"We have designed a comprehensive Meta rehabilitation program," President Kensington says. "All Metas will be trained to live normal lives as ordinary, productive members of society."

"Trained?" I say. "You mean, like animals?"

President Kensington smiles. "Need I remind you that I am the president of the United States of America? Just as you have dutifully upheld our laws in the past, I fully expect you to comply with our new law now. But if you foolishly choose to disobey, you will face the full power of the United States military. Just like your friends."

The camera pans back to Blue Bolt, Makeshift, and Master Mime who are still kneeling with their hands bound.

"I expect to see all of you at the Pentagon shortly," President Kensington says. "Or else."

Then, the monitor goes black.

"Well," Grace says, "that was unexpected."

"This is no time for jokes," Dad says. "We have to go to the Pentagon."

"What?" Mom says. "Are you crazy? We can't turn ourselves in."

"We're not turning ourselves in," Dad says. "We're rescuing our friends."

"Which is exactly what she is expecting," Shadow Hawk says. "It's a trap."

"Most likely," TechnocRat says. "But that's not the only thing worrying me. I'm still trying to figure out why Blue Bolt and the others are just sitting there like baked potatoes. Whatever is wrapped around their wrists must have some kind of a sedation effect. But I don't know anything that can do that."

Suddenly, green lights start flashing on the console.

"Hang on," TechnocRat says, typing into the keyboard. "We're getting a news alert."

Just then, the monitor flicks on again, but this time we're watching a live broadcast of a street mob. Thousands of people are pushing their way towards the city center, swarming five costumed individuals who are trying to walk down the street. What's going on? Then, a reporter comes into frame and starts speaking Japanese.

"Let me activate the translator," TechnocRat says.

Seconds later, we can understand the reporter in perfect English:

"… have complied peacefully with the request of the prime minister and are now in the hands of our military. Our once great Japanese champions are now prisoners of the government under the new Meta Restriction Resolution. We are not clear what the next steps are, but according to authorities, they will undergo a process called behavior modification. Details are coming in slowly…"

Japanese champions?

OMG! I know exactly who they are.

Suddenly, the crowd parts, and I recognize a masked man holding his arms in the air. It's the Green Dragon! And behind him are Tsunami, Fight Master, The Silent Samurai, and Zen! They're quickly surrounded by armored robots that look just like the Meta-Busters that President Kensington threatened us with, except these robots are painted red-and-white like the Japanese flag.

That's strange.

Why would we share military technology with Japan?

"Who are those guys?" Grace asks.

"They're the Rising Suns," I say. "The best superhero team in Japan. They helped me fight the Herald."

I shake my head in disbelief. Why would the Rising Suns surrender themselves to the government?

"And by the way," Grace says. "Didn't that reporter say something about 'behavior modification?' What's that?"

"Hold on," TechnocRat says. "There's another alert coming. This one is from Spain."

The image switches to another group of heroes surrendering to a different group of Meta-Busters, except these are painted red-and-yellow, like the Spanish flag.

"That's Los Toros," Shadow Hawk says. "The premier Spanish super team."

"The Meta Restriction Resolution has gone global," Mom says. "And heroes are turning themselves in."

"Yeah, the heroes are," TechnocRat says, "but what

about the villains?"

"This is nuts," Grace says. "Why do we bother saving these people if they don't even want us?"

"Because we're heroes," Dad says. "And it's our duty to protect the innocent, even if they're misguided. Now let's go save our friends."

"I can't wait," I say.

"Not you, Elliott," Dad says, putting his hand on my shoulder. "You're staying here."

"What?" I say. "But that's not fair!"

"Sorry, sucker," Grace says, flashing a big smile.

"You too, young lady," Mom says.

"What?" Grace protests, crossing her arms. "That's not fair either!"

"Now is not the time to argue," Dad says. "The political climate is too unstable. Plus, we don't know what those Meta-Busters are capable of. If they took out Blue Bolt, Master Mime, and Makeshift, then it's safer for you two to stay here. For everyone else—It's Fight Time!"

The heroes take off, except for Mom.

"Listen," she says. "This is serious business and we need you to stay put. I don't want to hear any nonsense about intergalactic kidnappings or time-traveling mishaps when I get back. Do I make myself clear?"

Grace and I look at one another.

"Do. I. Make. Myself. Clear?" Mom repeats.

"Yes," we say in harmony.

"Great," she says, kissing us on our foreheads. "I'm

expecting to see you both here, safe and sound, when we return."

Then, she shoots me a final look and leaves.

But as soon as we hear the last of Mom's footsteps fading down the hall, Grace turns and says—

"See ya, squirt!"

"What?" I say confused. "What's that supposed to mean?"

"It means I'm out of here," Grace says, unfolding her arms to reveal a pair of crossed fingers.

"Wait, you lied to Mom?" I say.

"Nope," she says. "I just had my fingers crossed."

"But that's the same thing as lying," I say.

"Is it?" she says, running off. "Oh, well. You snooze you lose!"

"But wait!" I yell. "You can't just—"

But apparently, she can.

Because she's gone.

And I'm all alone.

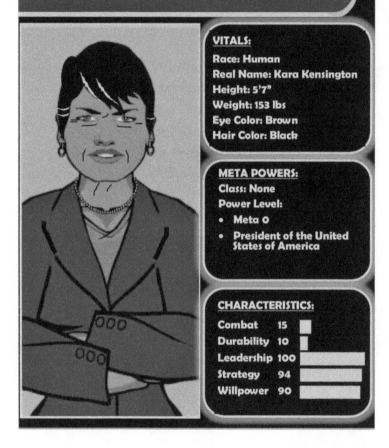

Meta Profile

Name: President Kensington
Role: Commander-in-Chief   Status: Active

VITALS:
Race: Human
Real Name: Kara Kensington
Height: 5'7"
Weight: 153 lbs
Eye Color: Brown
Hair Color: Black

META POWERS:
Class: None
Power Level:
- Meta 0
- President of the United States of America

CHARACTERISTICS:

Combat	15	▪
Durability	10	▪
Leadership	100	▬▬▬▬
Strategy	94	▬▬▬
Willpower	90	▬▬▬

THREE

I GET LEFT BEHIND... AGAIN

Well, I feel like a first-class loser.

I mean, I just stood here flat-footed while Grace raced off to help the team. And even though I want to follow her, I can't. After all, I promised Mom I wouldn't leave the Waystation.

Boy, I wish I crossed *my* fingers.

Oh well, at least I can watch the fireworks when Mom sees Grace on the battlefield. She's gonna flip!

But as soon as I head for the Monitor Room to catch the show, my stomach rumbles. I check the wall clock and realize why I'm so hungry. It's dinner time and I haven't eaten since well before my training debacle. Time sure flies when you're leading your team into disaster.

It should take the gang a few minutes to get to the Pentagon, so I've got time to grab a quick snack. But as I head towards the Galley, I hear noises.

Chewing noises.

Two thoughts hit me at once.

One, I remember I'm actually not alone. And two, I have the feeling I'm about to witness something ugly.

Like, really, really ugly.

When I finally reach the Galley, I brace myself and step inside. And then I wish I hadn't.

"Dog-Gone!" I yell. "Drop it!"

The big mutt is standing on the kitchen counter devouring a chicken drumstick. Diced carrots are scattered everywhere, and a half-eaten chicken carcass is resting comfortably in a fruit bowl.

Ugh! Mom must have just finished cooking when the call from the White House came in, and then she raced off and left everything behind.

The masked bandit strikes again.

"Get down!" I yell.

Dog-Gone looks at me wide-eyed.

"Oh, no you don't!" I warn. "No way! You will not turn invisible right now. Now drop the drumstick and help me clean this up."

But instead of stopping, he cocks an ear—and vanishes! Now all I see is the chicken drumstick, which leaps off the counter and bolts past me down the hallway.

Well, I can't say I'm surprised.

It's been quite a day. Not only did I screw up my chance of ever leading the Freedom Force again, but now I have to clean up after a rude German Shepherd with attitude problems.

I hope that chicken drumstick gives him gas.

I grab a paper towel and start picking up chunks of disgustingness when I suddenly remember what I was doing here in the first place. Ugh, all I wanted was a snack before the team leaped into action. Now I've probably missed the whole thing!

I toss what I'm holding into the garbage and hustle out of the Galley. So much for a bite to eat. Why does Dog-Gone get to feast while I'm still starving? Now I know why they call it 'a dog's world.'

I sprint down the hall and climb the twenty-three steps to the Monitor Room. Before I hop into the command chair, I take my grappling gun out of my utility belt because it tends to chafe my leg. Then, I sit down and punch a few codes into the keyboard. Seconds later, the screen blips on and I'm staring at the most famous five-sided building in the world.

The Pentagon.

Since I don't see any explosions, I'm guessing the team hasn't made their move yet. That's great news because it gives me time to do some reconnaissance. Maybe I can spot something up here that will help them down there.

I start by scouting the perimeter of the building.

Shadow Hawk said the Pentagon houses the Department of Defense, but that's about all I know. So, I query the system for some additional info. Seconds later, a bunch of facts scroll down the screen, like the Pentagon is the largest office building in the world at over six-and-a-half million square feet. Boy, I can't even imagine how many coffee stations are in there.

Of course, the building has five sides—hence, the name Pentagon. It also has five levels above ground and two known levels below ground. My eyes stop on the word 'known' and I wonder: if only two levels are known, how many are 'unknown?'

It's an interesting question, but I don't have time to dig into that now. Instead, I've got more important things to do, like figuring out why those restraints on my friends' wrists looked so familiar. But first I need a visual.

I set the telescopes on auto-zoom and cycle them around the building until I find what I'm looking for.

Ten seconds later, I've got it.

To my surprise, Blue Bolt, Master Mime, and Makeshift are still kneeling on the stairs out in the open. And hiding around the corner is a squad of Meta-Busters.

Yep, I'd definitely call that a trap.

I take a photo of Makeshift's wrists and lean in for a better look. Upon closer inspection, the restraints look rippled. I know I've seen a material like that before, but where?

Well, if anything can identify it, it'll be the Meta

Monitor. So, I feed it the image and hit the 'analyze' button.

This shouldn't take long.

In the meantime, I'd better call Dad and let him know what's going on. I don't want them to be ambushed.

"HQ to Captain Justice," I say, talking into the transmitter. "HQ to Captain Justice."

"Captain, here," Dad whispers back, but he doesn't sound happy. "Epic Zero, what are you doing? End this transmission now!"

"Hold on," I say. "I located the captives. They're on the Northeast side. And they're very well—"

"End the transmission now!" Dad whispers firmly.

"But why?" I ask. "I don't get it."

"Because we're at the Pentagon," Dad says. "And the Pentagon has the most advanced homing equipment in the world. Which means they'll pick up our connection and trace it to—"

"They found us!" I hear Mom yell in the background. "Get ready to fight!"

"Cut off!" Dad orders. "Before they find—"

Suddenly, there's a CLICK followed by STATIC.

Uh-oh.

I think I just got them in trouble. I mean, I was simply trying to help, but I screwed that up too. Sometimes I wonder why I even bother getting out of bed.

And what did Dad say at the end?

Cut off the transmission before they find… what?

"Alert! Alert! Alert!" the Meta Monitor blares.

Great. At least the Meta Monitor finished its analysis.

But when I look down at the screen I see:

MATERIAL ANALYSIS PENDING.

Huh? That's weird. If the Meta Monitor wasn't finished, then why did the alert—

"Waystation breached!" the Meta Monitor blares. "Automatic emergency response system activated! Repeat, Waystation breached! Automatic emergency response system activated!"

Huh? At first, I'm confused. And then my heart sinks to my toes because based on what it's saying, the Meta Monitor hadn't finished its analysis at all. Instead, it's telling me something different. It's saying that someone has boarded the Waystation!

But how?

And then it hits me.

Dad wasn't telling me to end the transmission to only protect *their* location! He was telling me to end the transmission to also protect *my* location!

And the last time the Waystation was invaded I ended up being kidnapped by a talking chimpanzee! There ain't no way I'm letting that happen again!

I've got to get out of here!

I'm about to slide off my chair when I see:

ANALYSIS STATUS: 65% COMPLETE.

I stop.

I mean, I desperately want to know what those restraints are made of, but I can't just stay here like a sitting duck. I glance back down at the monitor.

75% COMPLETE.

It's almost done. If I can just hang on for a few more seconds I'll know what—

BOOM!

Suddenly, the whole Waystation shakes violently and I grip the arms of the command chair for dear life!

That wasn't good! Not good at all!

85% COMPLETE.

I exhale. I just need a few more—

KABOOM!

The Waystation shakes harder this time and a blue wire springs loose from the Meta Monitor's console. Okay, I definitely need to get out of here. Especially since that one sounded way closer! I glance at the screen.

95% COMPLETE.

C'mon! So close!

Then, I hear a BARK.

Dog-Gone!

That does it! I leap from the chair and rush down the steps. Look, I want those results more than anything, but not if Dog-Gone is in danger! But when I reach the bottom I'm blocked by a gate!

The Meta Monitor initiated its response sequence!

I run through TechnocRat's override codes in my head. The first one I remember is for the residential wing.

Then the Combat Room. Darn it! These codes are so similar I'm mixing them up in my head. I'm losing time. C'mon, think!

Maybe this one?

"Override ZY7889ZZ," I yell.

The gate retracts into the ceiling.

Yes! Things are finally going my way. But when I pop into the corridor, I freeze. Because something huge is staring at me from down the hall. Something with red, unblinking eyes.

It's... a Meta-Buster?

Here on the Waystation?

But my powers don't work on robots.

"PRIME TARGET IDENTIFIED," the Meta-Buster says in a deep, mechanical voice. "PER PRESIDENTIAL ORDER, CAPTURE ALIVE. DO NOT DAMAGE."

Um, did it just say, 'presidential order?'

Then, it raises its arm and my alarm bells go off. I press myself flat against the wall just as a net whips past my face. Okay, I'm no zoo animal. It's time to move!

I somersault across the hall into the next corridor, pop up on my feet, and book it. With that bucket of bolts up here, there's no way I can stay on the Waystation.

And then I get a disturbing thought.

What if there's more than—

SMACK!

I stumble backward, my nose throbbing. But before I

can regain my wits, something grabs me by my arms and lifts me into the air. The next thing I know, I'm staring into the electronic eyes of another Meta-Buster!

"Let me go!" I yell.

"PRIME TARGET CAPTURED ALIVE," it says.

I kick it with my foot but it's like kicking a truck. There's no give! Plus, it's squeezing my arms so tight they're going numb!

I can't believe it. How could I give away both of our locations in the same boneheaded move? I try breaking free again but the Meta-Buster is too strong. And even if I did get away, the Waystation is probably crawling with these things.

There's nothing I can do.

I'm caught.

And then I see a chicken coming towards me.

Or rather, a chicken carcass?

At first, I think I'm imagining things, but then I realize what's going on. That's no runaway chicken carcass—it's my invisible pooch Dog-Gone—and he's heading this way!

The next thing I know, Dog-Gone uses the Meta-Buster's metallic backside like a vault and leaps up, jamming the chicken carcass over the robot's head!

"SURPRISE ATTACK!" it says, dropping me hard to the ground as it tries to remove its poultry helmet.

Just then, Dog-Gone materializes in front of me and pulls me to my feet with his mouth.

"Yuck," I say. "Chicken breath."

That's gross, but right now I've got to focus on more important things, like staying alive.

"This way!" I yell, sprinting towards the Hangar.

If my calculations are correct, Blue Bolt took one Freedom Flyer and Dad took the other. So, if those vehicles are gone and Grace followed them in a Freedom Ferry, then that means there should be one Freedom Ferry left. But if I'm wrong, I've trapped us in the Hangar with nowhere to go.

It's a gamble, but it's our only chance.

Suddenly, a laser zips past us, exploding into the wall.

Um, what happened to capturing me alive?

"Keep moving, boy!" I yell.

We round the corner as a barrage of lasers tear up the wall behind us. But suddenly, a massive robot steps out and grabs my cape, lifting me off my feet!

"PRIME TARGET CAPTURED ALIVE," it says.

Not again!

"DESTROY PRIME TARGET," comes a different voice from down the hall.

Um, what?

But before I can react, a laser plows right through the eye of the Meta-Buster holding me, and it falls backward, sparks flying from its eye socket.

I land on my feet next to Dog-Gone and look back.

More Meta-Busters are on our tail! And for some reason, they destroyed one of their own!

"Into the Hangar!" I yell.

We motor inside and I thank my lucky stars because sitting in the very last parking spot is a Freedom Ferry!

"Go for it!" I instruct Dog-Gone.

He's there in a flash—the benefit of four legs—and pops the hatch. I catch up and hop inside, crashing into Dog-Gone who is hogging the seat.

"Move your big rump," I say, taking the controls.

But the Meta-Busters are right behind us! There's no way we'll get this out of here without them spotting us.

Wait a second. Spotting us?

I may not be able to copy the Meta-Buster's powers, but I can copy Dog-Gone's invisibility power. I concentrate hard, pulling in his Meta energy, and then I push it out, covering me, Dog-Gone, and the Freedom Ferry in a cloak of invisibility.

And none too soon, as five Meta-Busters spill into the Hangar looking around confused.

Hah! Those morons will never find us. Time to jet.

But when I turn on the Freedom Ferry, the engine lets out a thunderous VROOOM!

Seriously? Whoever drove this last must have taken it off of 'Silent Mode.' I'm guessing it was Master Mime.

"Um, you don't think they heard that, do you?" I whisper to Dog-Gone. But I already know the answer.

"ACTIVATE INFRARED VISION," a Meta-Buster calls out, its voice echoing through the Hangar.

Infrared vision? As in, heat-seeking vision?

"Get ready!" I warn Dog-Gone, strapping us in.

"DESTROY PRIME TARGET."

I punch it.

The Freedom Ferry blasts off, throwing Dog-Gone and me backward. I press the door opener and grip the steering wheel tight, trying to maintain control as we fishtail left and right towards the slowly opening door.

Then, I look in the rearview mirror.

The Meta-Busters have positioned themselves behind us, pointing their arms in our direction. Holy cow, they're gunning for us! They're going to fire at us!

"DESTROY PRIME TARGET," one repeats.

"Hold on to your biscuits, Dog-Gone!"

I slam the gas pedal, and bash the door opener again, signaling it to close. The Freedom Ferry lurches forward at maximum speed and I hear Dog-Gone's ears snap back.

I'd better time this right or we're roadkill!

I peek into the sideview mirror as smoke rises from the Meta-Busters' hands, but we speed through the opening just as the door SLAMS shut behind us.

THOOM!!!

There's a massive explosion from behind, knocking the Freedom Ferry off course. Something hits the back of our vehicle hard and the dashboard lights up. Great. One of the thrusters is out of order, but the other is okay.

I breathe a sigh of relief.

Wow, that was crazy. I can't believe we made it. I

mean, those Meta-Busters were really trying to kill us. I just hope the Waystation wasn't too badly damaged.

But when I check the rearview mirror, my jaw drops.

Because the Waystation is gone.

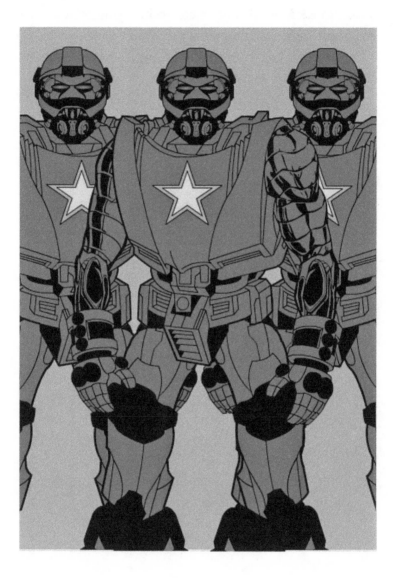

FOUR

I CRASH-LAND INTO ANOTHER FINE MESS

I'm in complete and total shock.

The entire Waystation, our headquarters and home, was just blown to smithereens by a squad of psycho Meta-Busters! Everything we own, everything we care about, is now space dust.

I feel like I'm gonna hurl.

I mean, it's mind-boggling to think about everything we've just lost. The Meta Monitor. GISMO. All of our Meta gear. The memorial statues in the Hall of Fallen Heroes. Dog-Gone's puppy pictures. My comic books.

They're all gone.

And it's all my fault.

None of this would have happened if I hadn't called Dad. And speaking of Dad, he's gonna kill me when he comes home from the Pentagon and there is no more home! And he's not the only one!

I can't even imagine Grace's reaction when she sees that all of her stuff is vaporized. And poor TechnocRat is going to flip his whiskers when he realizes his lab is gone.

OMG!

TechnocRat's stash of Camembert cheese is gone too!

He's gonna nibble me to death!

But just to add more salt to my wounds, it doesn't look like I can even warn them, because the blast that knocked out one of the Freedom Ferry's thrusters also knocked out the communications system. And based on the red light flashing in my face, the landing gear is on the fritz too.

Just. Freaking. Wonderful.

Dog-Gone and I were lucky to get out of the Waystation alive, but we might eat it trying to land this sucker. And since we only have one thruster, I'm not sure we'll have enough juice to make it to the Pentagon. When I enter Earth's atmosphere, I'm going to have to touchdown somewhere closer, like Keystone City.

I plug in the coordinates and rest my head in my hands. I feel like such a heel. Maybe I should have let those Meta-Busters capture me. But then again, the whole thing was pretty confusing.

That first Meta-Buster said it had a presidential order to capture me alive, but the other ones didn't seem to get the memo. Instead, they were clearly trying to kill me, and even destroyed one of their own to do it!

I don't know what to make of that, but I do know one thing. This is, without a doubt, the worst day ever.

The only good thing I managed to do was take Dog-Gone with me. My apologies to TechnocRat, but nearly everything else on the Waystation can be rebuilt. Dog-Gone, however, is one of a kind.

Except right now the poor guy is panting heavily and whimpering under his breath. I need to be brave for him.

"It's gonna be okay," I say, rubbing his back. "Let's just land this Freedom Ferry safely."

But deep down I know that's going to be easier said than done. As soon as I get a visual on Keystone City, I hit the 'Extend Landing Gear' button and pray, but all I hear is WHIRRING. I try again and hear the same result—which officially confirms it. The landing gear is stuck.

Why am I not surprised?

My heart is racing but I need to stay calm. Unfortunately, we can't just eject because the seats on the Freedom Ferry aren't equipped with jets like the seats on the Freedom Flyer. So, this is pretty much going to be a legit emergency landing.

Luckily, I've practiced emergency landings a few times in the flight simulator, but I've never actually done

one for real. Well, I guess there's no time like the present!

"Hold on," I say. "This is gonna get bumpy."

I call up a map of Keystone City to find the best possible landing spot for a 50,000-pound spacecraft without the ability to stop itself. After a quick scan of the topography, I realize I'm going to need a pretty long runway to slow my momentum.

So that only leaves one option: Main Street.

Fortunately, it's well after rush hour so there shouldn't be many cars on the road. At least, I hope not. But as I grip the steering column, I realize my hands are soaked. Yuck, I'm so nervous I'm actually sweating through my gloves.

I glance over at Dog-Gone who is covering his eyes with his paws. Now there's a vote of confidence.

Time to focus.

The streetlamps lining the road light up Main Street like a landing strip, so I just need to stay within the lines and hope there's no traffic. Thankfully, it looks clear as we approach, so I pull back on the column and dive in.

Within seconds we touch down. I angle the Freedom Ferry to land the rear first, resulting in an ear-piercing SCREECH as tungsten steel scrapes against concrete. Then, I lay down the front, throwing Dog-Gone and I forward. Sparks fly all around us as we skid along the street, seemingly forever.

But I have other ideas.

I call up the wing propulsion system and spin the

dial, reversing my one working thruster. Then, I punch the "Thrust" button, and the jet kicks on, slowing our momentum. But because all of our power is on the left side, we swerve off-balance. I counter with the steering column, but it takes another five thousand feet or so until we come to a complete stop.

I breathe a sigh of relief.

"See," I say to Dog-Gone. "That wasn't so—"

HOOONNNKKK!

SCREEEECCCCHHHHH!

My eyes bug out as I see two giant headlights heading straight for us! Instinctively, I grab Dog-Gone's collar, but there's no time to get out! So, I throw my body over Dog-Gone and brace for impact.

PSSSSHHHHHH!

Seconds later, I'm still gritting my teeth.

Huh? Where's the impact?

Dog-Gone and I look at one another, and then I poke my head up to find a huge truck stopped only inches away from the Freedom Ferry.

"What are you doing, kid?" the driver yells, leaning out of his cab. "You could have killed somebody!"

"Sorry," I say. "We just... dropped in?"

"Crazy city drivers!" he yells. And then he backs up his truck and goes around us, shaking his fist at me.

Well, that was lucky. But he's right about one thing, we're sitting in the middle of a four-way intersection. I reverse the wing thruster and motor us over to the side of the road. There, that should handle that, but based on all of the sputtering coming from the engine, this might have been the Freedom Ferry's last ride.

"C'mon, boy," I say, popping the hatch.

We climb out of the Freedom Ferry and look around. Honestly, I've never felt so lost before. I mean, I've got no home, no transportation, and no clue what to do next. Then, I notice we're parked in front of a storefront with televisions in the window. The sign above the window reads: *Keystone City Electronics Emporium*. My eyes drift back to the TVs when I realize they're tuned in to the news. Maybe I can get some info?

I hustle over to the window to find a female news anchor talking to camera with some words scrolling beneath her that read: *Freedom Force Captured!*

Oh. No.

Suddenly, the image jumps to Dad being held down by a group of Meta-Busters. And they're wrapping his wrists with those mysterious leather straps! Then, there's another image showing a group of Meta-Busters carrying away the rest of the team, including Mom and Grace!

Ugh! I was hoping Grace stayed out of it, but it looks like she couldn't help herself. Now they're all prisoners—except for me.

Just then, I feel something wet nuzzle into my palm.

Well, me and Dog-Gone.

But I still can't believe it.

We're the only heroes left.

"Hey, kid," comes a man's voice from behind that makes me jump out of my skin. "Are you taking those?"

I spin around to find a masked, mustached man wearing a blue costume with the insignia of vapor on his chest. Immediately, I know who he is.

"Y-You're Mr. Mister," I say.

"Yeah," he says. "And who are you, the Queen of England?"

For a second, I'm stunned. I mean, Mr. Mister is a Meta 3 villain who can evaporate solid objects into pure mist! I've never faced him before, but I've read his Meta profile and he's one tough customer.

"Now are you claiming those or not?" he asks.

"Um, claiming what?" I say.

"Those TV's," he says. "You got here first so I'm trying to be polite. Now, I'll ask you one last time. Are you looting them or not?"

Looting them?

"You mean, like, stealing them?" I ask.

"Yeah," he says. "There ain't no more heroes around so you can take whatever you want. Everyone's doing it."

Um, everyone?

Suddenly, I hear a CRASH and when I look to my right, I do a double take, because dozens of costumed criminals are stampeding down Main Street! I see Slap Stick and Ferret King and Dark Mind and so on and so forth.

It's like a field day for Meta villains!

"Scoot over," Mr. Mister says, putting his hands on the glass window. Then, he furrows his brow, and seconds later the glass is gone!

He evaporated it into thin air!

"I'm taking this one," he says, grabbing a flat-screen TV. "I accidentally vaporized my last one."

Dog-Gone bares his teeth and I grab his collar before he lurches forward.

"Stay," I whisper.

Believe me, I'd love nothing more than to stop Mr. Mister, but if he doesn't know we're the good guys, then it probably isn't the best time to announce it to the world. Especially if Main Street is crawling with criminals. For the moment, our best option is to lay low. There's no reason to blow our cover over a silly television.

"Return that television, crook!" comes a girl's voice.

Huh?

Suddenly, a heinous odor assaults my nostrils and I cringe. It smells like rotten eggs and spoiled meat all rolled into one barf-inducing package. I pinch my nose, but not before I start feeling queasy.

"What's that smell?" Mr. Mister says, looking like he's about to heave.

Just then, a masked girl wearing a black costume with a white stripe down the center appears on the scene.

"I warned you, creep!" she says. "Now put back that television or face the wrath of Skunk Girl!"

Um, did she just call herself 'Skunk Girl?'

"Go take a bath," Mr. Mister says, ignoring her.

"Get 'em, Pinball!" Skunk Girl yells.

The next thing I know, a round, gray object bigger than a boulder bounces over our heads and SLAMS into Mr. Mister, knocking the TV right out of his hands. The flat screen falls and SHATTERS on the ground.

"My TV!" Mr. Mister cries out.

And that's when I realize that bouncy, round object is no object, it's another costumed kid!

"Whoops," Pinball says. "Sorry."

"Oh, I'll make you sorry," Mr. Mister says, rising to his feet. "By evaporating you!" But just as he's about to grab Pinball, there's a blinding flash of white light and I'm suddenly seeing stars.

"Nice shot, Selfie," Skunk Girl says.

Selfie?

When my vision finally clears, I find Mr. Mister rubbing his eyes and a pretty girl with a brown ponytail and a sleek white-and-silver costume staring at her phone.

"Thanks," she says, looking up at me with her bright, blue eyes. "I can't wait to post it."

These kids look like they're my age.

"Um, pardon me," I say, "but who are you people?"

"Oh, we're Next Gen," Skunk Girl says proudly.

"Next Gen?" I say. "What's that mean?"

"It means we're the Next Gen," she says, "As in 'the Next Generation' of Meta heroes."

"Yeah," Pinball says. "We met in a chat room."

"So," Skunk Girl says, looking me up and down, "I take it you're a villain too. Ready for a bashing?"

"Um, no," I answer. "I'm a hero. But you do know that Meta heroes are banned, right? I mean, I appreciate what you're trying to do, but it's not a great time to be running around in public right now."

"Don't worry about us, buddy," Skunk Girl says. "It may be our first mission, but we can handle ourselves."

Their first mission? I swallow hard.

"Wait a second!" Selfie says. "I know you. I streamed your interview on the CNC Morning Newsflash. You're a member of the Freedom Force. Epic Zebra, right?"

"Shhh!" I whisper. "I am a member of the Freedom Force, but my name isn't—"

"Hey!" Mr. Mister calls out. "Hey, everyone! Get this, that kid in the red-and-blue is a superhero. And he's a member of the Freedom Force!"

Oh, jeez! So much for laying low.

"The Freedom Force?" comes a voice from down the street. "Where?"

"President Kensington offered a reward for bringing in a kid named Epic Zero," comes another voice. "A big one!"

Wait, what? A reward? For me?

Suddenly, there's a mob of villains heading our way.

"Did I say something wrong?" Selfie asks.

"Yeah," I say. "Kind of."

"Sorry," she says.

But her apology comes too late because seconds later, we're surrounded.

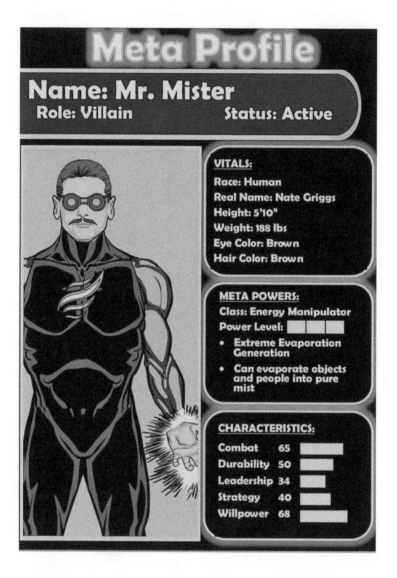

Meta Profile

Name: Mr. Mister
Role: Villain   Status: Active

VITALS:

Race: Human
Real Name: Nate Griggs
Height: 5'10"
Weight: 188 lbs
Eye Color: Brown
Hair Color: Brown

META POWERS:

Class: Energy Manipulator
Power Level: ▮▮▮
- **Extreme Evaporation Generation**
- **Can evaporate objects and people into pure mist**

CHARACTERISTICS:

Combat	65	
Durability	50	
Leadership	34	
Strategy	40	
Willpower	68	

FIVE

I GET A BABYSITTING GIG

I really didn't need this right now.

I mean, my bad decisions have already cost me my family and my home. Shouldn't that be enough for one day? But I guess the answer is 'no,' because I'm now surrounded by a mob of Meta villains who want to turn me over to President Kensington for a big reward.

And to top it off, I'm also babysitting—

"Um, where did all of these villains come from?" Pinball asks. "And which one isn't wearing deodorant?"

—three amateur heroes.

"Get that kid," Mr. Mister says, pointing at me. "He must be Epic Zero. He's the one the president wants."

"Whoa, chill," I say, trying to sound calm. "Everyone just relax. You've got the wrong guy here. My name is

Epic Zebra. I know I look just like Epic Zero, but trust me, I'm not. Besides, everyone knows how easy it is to get Metas confused. Remember when Captain Justice took out Devil Head thinking it was Head Devil? Poor Devil Head was just going for a manicure, but cases of mistaken identity happen all the time in our business. So, how about we skip the unnecessary fight scene and jump to the part where we make up and you buy me ice cream?"

"There ain't gonna be no making up," says a short villain with two humungous eyes. "I saw you on that CNC morning news show and I know you're Epic Zero."

"Yeah," Slap Stick says. "Flashback never forgets a face. If he says you're Epic Zero, then you're Epic Zero."

Flashback? That's Flashback?

Uh-oh. Flashback has the ability to retain everything he's ever seen. So, he knows I'm really me—and now so does everyone else!

"So, what are you saying?" I ask. "No ice cream?"

"Oh, I'll make ice cream," Mr. Mister says, raising his hands. "Out of you!"

I do some quick math. There are twenty-one of them and five of us. Even if I negate Mr. Mister's powers, we don't have the firepower to take them all in a fair fight. What's that other old saying—he that fights and runs away, may live to fight another day?

"Guys," I whisper to Next Gen, "grab me if you want to live."

As multiple hands wrap around my arms and a furry body presses against my leg, I get down to business. With all of these Metas around, I've got plenty of options. But I decide to keep it simple.

First, I borrow Dog-Gone's invisibility power.

"Hey!" Mr. Mister says. "Where did they go?"

Then, I grab Slap Stick's adhesion power, making my skin super-clingy so my new friends stick to me like glue.

Finally, I copy Pinball's power, and my body suddenly expands like a balloon, which is accompanied by a loud RIPPING sound as the fabric splits from the bottom of my pants.

Awesome.

But I can't worry about that now because I've got to get us out of here!

"Hold on tight!" I say.

I do a little jump, and when my feet touch the ground, we spring into the air like a super-charged bouncy ball. In fact, we're so high the villains down below look like ants and Selfie lets out a blood-curdling scream, but I think it's kind of fun.

That is, until I realize everyone looking up can see my Batman-logoed underpants. But then I remember we're still invisible and breathe a sigh of relief.

And with my next bounce, we're long gone.

***

Twenty minutes later, we're sitting on the floor of a treehouse in the backyard of a suburban home. It's dark out and the crickets are chirping away, blissfully unaware of the chaos happening in the world around them.

"Cheese puffs?" Selfie offers, holding out a bag.

"Thanks," I say, grabbing a bunch. But as soon as I pull my hand out, a large snout invades my palm and sucks up all of the goodies. Sometimes I wonder if my dog is actually a dog or a vacuum cleaner covered in fur.

"Should he really be eating those?" Pinball asks.

"Definitely not," I say, "but unless you've got dog treats up here, I'll let it go this time. He's had a pretty rough day."

"Me too," Pinball says, adjusting his position. He's so round he can't fit comfortably into any corner. "Hey, Selfie, what's a guy gotta do around here to get some cheese puffs?"

"Don't be rude," Selfie says, offering me the bag again. "We serve our guests first. Besides, you'd probably eat the whole bag all by yourself."

"Hey!" Pinball says, raising his index finger. "I resemble that remark."

I take out another handful and stuff them into my mouth before Dog-Gone has a chance to steal them away. Then, I take a look around.

From the outside, the treehouse looked pretty normal, complete with a rickety old ladder, but the inside is way more sophisticated than I imagined. One wall is covered with floor-to-ceiling computers and giant maps of Keystone City. Another wall holds a large bookshelf with all kinds of supplies on it, like water bottles, tools, and a first aid kit. It's pretty impressive for a treehouse, but it's no Waystation.

"So," I say, talking with my mouth full, "is this, like, your headquarters?"

"Yeah," Skunk Girl says. "Why? Is it not good enough for you?"

"Skunk Girl!" Selfie says.

"It's great," I say. "You've got everything you need here. Speaking of which, do you happen to have a sewing kit? I seem to have split my... I mean, I need to repair my costume."

"Sure," Selfie says, pulling a plastic box off of the shelf. "Here it is. Do you need help?"

"Um, no thanks," I say, my face going flush. "I've got it. But I'd appreciate it if you guys could turn away for a few minutes while I take care of some, um, personal business."

"Oh," Selfie says, her eyebrows raised. "Got it."

"Seriously?" Skunk Girl says. "Fine."

They both turn around.

"I can't move but I'll close my eyes," Pinball says.

I'm all set, except for one last pair of peepers.

"You too," I tell Dog-Gone.

He rolls his eyes and turns away.

Then, I drop my pants and get to work. Yep, just as I

thought, it's a pretty big tear. Thankfully, Dad taught me how to sew. He said Meta heroes have to be prepared for anything, and boy was he right!

"You know," Pinball says. "What you did back there was really cool. You've got some major powers."

"No kidding, Pinball," Selfie says. "He's on the Freedom Force for goodness sake. Of course he's got major powers."

"Well, thanks," I say, threading as quickly as I can. "I'm just doing my job."

"We didn't need him, you know," Skunk Girl says. "We could have taken them ourselves."

"Are you crazy?" Pinball says. "There were hundreds of villains out there."

"Twenty-one," I say. "Not that I was counting."

"Right," Pinball says. "But that's the point. You know because you have more caped crusading experience in your little pinkie than all of us put together. We could learn a lot from you. In fact, Selfie and I were talking, and we think you'd make a great leader for Next Gen."

"What?" Skunk Girl and I say simultaneously.

"Um, I'm no leader," I say.

"But I wanted to be our leader," Skunk Girl says, clearly frustrated.

"You will be," Selfie says, putting her hand on Skunk Girl's shoulder. "But we have to be honest with ourselves and we could have been killed out there. If he can teach us the ropes, then we'll be able to handle any situation."

"Hmph!" Skunk Girl remarks. "I'm not buying it."

"Look," I say, putting my pants back on, "I'm flattered, but I'm really not a good leader. Oh, and you guys can turn around now."

"You're wrong," Pinball says, opening his eyes. "You're not a good leader, you're a great leader. I mean, you saved all of us back there."

"That was dumb luck," I say. "Who knows if I could do that again. Trust me, if you saw the day I've had, you'd pay me not to be your leader."

"Stop pressuring him," Skunk Girl says. "He's clearly not interested. He thinks he's better than us."

"What?" I say. "No, I don't think that at all. I've just got a lot going on. And you shouldn't even be out there right now. President Kensington has banned all Metas, and here's a newsflash for you—that includes you guys. If her Meta-Busters catch you, you're doomed."

"Just like the Freedom Force?" Pinball asks.

My mouth opens but no words come out. I mean, how do I respond to that? The Freedom Force was captured because of me. And if I tell Next Gen it was my fault, what will they think of me then?

"Yes," I finally say. "Just like the Freedom Force."

"But you're going to save them," Selfie says. "Aren't you?"

"Well, of course he is," Pinball says.

"I... I...," I stammer.

"And you want this guy to lead us?" Skunk Girl says.

"Listen," I say, "I am planning on saving them. I just don't know how."

"Why don't you talk to the president?" Selfie asks.

"The president?" I say. "The president of the United States? She's the one causing all of this madness."

"Exactly," Selfie says. "If you can convince her to repeal the Meta Restriction Resolution, then all of this hero targeting will go away."

At first, what she's saying seems ridiculous. But the more I think about it, the more it makes perfect sense. I mean, I could try breaking into the Pentagon to rescue my family, but with all of those Meta-Busters around it would be a suicide mission. But instead, if I can simply convince President Kensington that she's wrong about Metas, I could solve everything once and for all.

"That's a great idea," I say. "But there's just one problem. How am I supposed to get inside the White House? After all, I'm a Meta. Even if I use Dog-Gone's invisibility power, the Meta-Busters could spot me with their infrared vision."

It's quiet for a minute, and then…

"You know," Pinball says, breaking the silence, "they have tours of the White House all the time. My brother's fifth-grade class went last year. If we're lucky, maybe there's a tour we can crash tomorrow."

It's actually not a bad idea, except for one thing.

"I like it," I say, "but there's no *we*. There's just me, and my dog. We'll do this on our own."

"Well, that sounds great to me," Skunk Girl says, gesturing to the ladder. "Why don't I show you the way out?"

"Knock it off, Skunk Girl," Selfie says, taking the sewing kit back. "Look, Epic Zero, you're going to need help. I mean, we've been helpful so far, right?"

"Well, yeah," I admit.

"Great," she says. "Then maybe you could use more help. Tell you what, why don't you think about it tonight? You can sleep right here in the treehouse."

Well, I am tired. And Dog-Gone looks exhausted.

Selfie pulls a blanket off the shelf and hands it to me.

"Thanks," I say. "But wait, where are you guys sleeping?"

"Oh," Selfie says. "We're in my backyard. That's my house right there. Skunk Girl is sleeping over, but don't worry, you won't be alone, because Pinball can bunk out here with you."

"It'll be awesome," Pinball says with a wink. "I've got loads of questions."

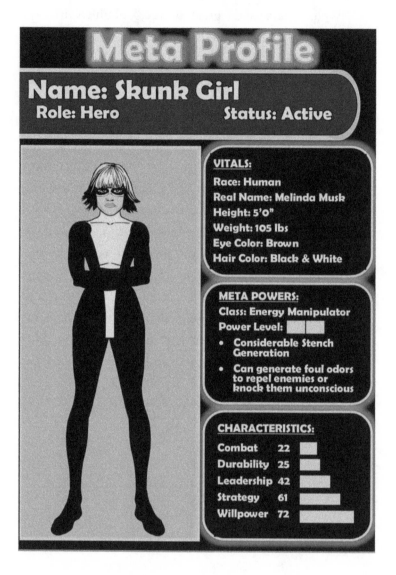

Meta Profile

Name: Skunk Girl
Role: Hero   **Status: Active**

VITALS:

Race: Human
Real Name: Melinda Musk
Height: 5'0"
Weight: 105 lbs
Eye Color: Brown
Hair Color: Black & White

META POWERS:

Class: Energy Manipulator
Power Level:

- Considerable Stench Generation
- Can generate foul odors to repel enemies or knock them unconscious

CHARACTERISTICS:

Combat	22	
Durability	25	
Leadership	42	
Strategy	61	
Willpower	72	

SIX

I CATCH THE BUS

Note to self: never, ever, E-V-E-R, sleep in the same room as Pinball again.

The dude talked non-stop until I literally had to pretend I was sleeping. And then, once he finally stopped talking, he snored like a chainsaw all night long! I didn't sleep a wink and based on Dog-Gone's droopy eyes, he didn't either.

But truthfully, I'm not sure it mattered. There are so many thoughts spinning inside my head I probably wouldn't have slept anyway. Of course, destroying the Waystation is weighing on my mind. But the biggest thing I can't shake is how I got my family captured.

If something happens to them because of me I don't know what I'll do. I just hope they're not undergoing 'behavior modification,' whatever that is.

Then, I keep debating if I should go to the White House alone or not. I mean, there's really no reason to drag Next Gen into this mess. Besides, they're rookies. What if they got captured—or worse? That settles it, I have to go solo. I can't risk their lives too.

But as soon as I throw off my blanket, I catch Dog-Gone's tired eyes. The poor lug. If I don't take him with me, he'll probably never sleep again.

"C'mon, boy," I whisper, as sunlight streams through the treehouse planks. Maybe I can make my getaway before anyone wakes up. But just as I tiptoe over to the ladder, Selfie appears.

"Where are you going?" she asks, pulling herself up and into the treehouse. That's when I notice she's wearing a blue backpack.

"Um, Dog-Gone has to use the bathroom," I say, lying through my teeth. "He's got a really small bladder."

"Uh-huh," she says, eyeing me suspiciously. Then, she nudges Pinball with her foot. "Wake up, Pinball."

"Huh?" Pinball snorts as drool rolls down his chin.

"Here," she says, pressing something into my hand. "That's your White House tour ticket."

My White House tour ticket? That's impossible. But when I look down at the ticket, it reads:

- *Official White House Tour Ticket*
- *Name: Bruce Wayne*
- *Age: 12*

- *Citizenship: United States of America*
- *Gender: Male*
- *City of Residence: Keystone City*

Okay, now I'm totally confused. I mean, it looks like a real White House Tour ticket, but I thought you had to write your Congressman months in advance to get one.

"Um, how did you get this?" I ask. "And why does it say I'm 'Bruce Wayne?' That's Batman's secret identity."

"Well, now it's you," she says. "I created them on the computer. Someone posted a picture of what a tour ticket looks like, so I made one for each of us. My mom is a graphic designer, so I used her design software and then printed them on cardstock. Not too shabby, huh?"

"Hey, I'm Clark Kent!" Pinball says, proudly holding up his ticket.

"Right," I say. "Look, these tickets are impressive, but they're not going to fool anyone. I'm sure there's a special hologram or something we're missing. Plus, we're not even signed up on the official White House tour list."

"Oh, don't worry about that," Selfie says with a sly smile. "When we get there just leave it to me. Now get changed."

She tosses me the blue backpack and I open it up to find a bundle of clothing. There's a red t-shirt, blue jeans, socks, and a pair of sneakers.

"Who are these for?" I ask.

"For you, Bruce Wayne," she says, getting back onto the ladder. "What? Did you think we'd just waltz into the

White House in our costumes? We need to look like normal kids. Those clothes belong to my younger brother and you looked about the same size. Get changed and I'll meet you guys on the ground in about ten minutes."

"Younger brother?" I mutter, but she's already gone.

Well, I guess she's right about one thing, no Meta-Buster worth its sensors is going to let us enter the White House dressed as superheroes. But as soon as I start removing my mask, I freeze. What am I doing?

If I take off my mask, these kids will see my face!

That's a major 'no-no!'

But then again, what other choice do I have? The Freedom Ferry is kaput and it's not like I can sneak into the White House using Dog-Gone's invisibility power. Those Meta-Busters have infrared vision! So, I guess Selfie's plan is the only plan I've got.

I breathe deeply and take off my mask.

"Ha!" Pinball chuckles.

"What's so funny?" I ask.

"Well," he says, "with your mask on, I didn't realize you actually had eyebrows."

"Gee," I say. "That's hysterical."

Then, I turn my back and put on Selfie's brother's clothing. Fortunately, it fits, and when I'm done dressing, I stuff my costume and utility belt into the backpack and throw it over my shoulder.

"Let's go, Dog-Gone," I say, descending the ladder.

Dog-Gone follows, but when he looks over the edge

of the treehouse, he suddenly backs up.

"Get back here you big baby," I say. "Climb down backward like I did. Don't worry, I'll support you."

After a few seconds, Dog-Gone extends his business end over the edge, and then lowers a back paw down gingerly until it finds its footing on the ladder. Then comes another paw. And then another. And the next thing I know, his rump is pressed squarely onto my face.

Just. Freaking. Wonderful.

We climb down slowly, and when we finally reach the bottom, my nose is relieved.

"Well, that was graceful," Skunk Girl says, her arms crossed. She's not wearing her mask either and is dressed in all black with a t-shirt that reads: *Punk Rock Rules*. She's also wearing a black-and-white backpack which I assume is holding her costume.

"Hey," comes Selfie's voice from behind.

But when I turn around, I inadvertently gasp, because she's not wearing her mask either and I can see her face—which is, well, really pretty. She's staring at me with her blue eyes and has her hair in a long braid.

"Are you okay?" she asks. "You look really red."

"Um, me?" I stammer. "Oh… yeah. I'm good. Real good." Why am I rambling like a dork?

"Great," she says. "But you do know your dog is peeing on our headquarters, right?"

"What?" I say, turning to find Dog-Gone standing at the base of the tree with his hind leg in the air.

"Dog-Gone!" I yell. "Really?"

"Let's bounce!" Pinball says, dropping from the sky and landing between us. His headgear is off and he's wearing a blue tracksuit with yellow stripes.

"Sounds good," Selfie says. "But this time we're not gonna bounce, we're gonna roll. We've got a bus to catch."

***

"Get your flea-bitten butt off of me," I whisper to Dog-Gone, who is wedged on the floor of the bus between my knees and the seat in front of me.

I feel his weight lift off my feet, but then he plops down again, crushing my toes. Well, he's clearly not going to budge, not that he has anywhere else to go because every seat is taken. Thankfully, he's invisible, otherwise, we never would have gotten him onto the bus in the first place. So, I guess I've got no choice but to grin and bear his weight for our three-hour ride to Washington D.C.

Lucky me.

At least I managed to avoid sitting next to Pinball. Talk about squished! Instead, I'm next to Selfie in the back of the bus, which is presenting, well... different challenges.

I mean, how come my stomach does flips every time I look at her? And why can't I even get up the nerve to talk to her? We've been sitting in awkward silence ever since the bus started moving.

Okay, I've got to say something. Maybe I'll ask her what her favorite color is. No, that's lame. Maybe her favorite food. No, that's really lame. Maybe—

"I'm sorry about your friends," she says suddenly.

"What food is your favorite color?" I blurt out.

"Huh?" she says, staring at me like I have two heads.

"Um, nothing," I say. Why am I such a goober? "Sorry, what did you say?"

"I said I'm sorry about your friends," she says. "You know, the Freedom Force?"

"Oh, those friends," I say, totally embarrassed. "Of course. Yeah, I-I hope they're okay."

As I look out the window at the passing trees, I flashback to the image of my family being carted away by Meta-Busters. I still can't believe it was my fault. And I never did find out what those leathery straps were.

Suddenly, I feel someone tapping on my right arm.

"Huh?" I say, turning to find Selfie staring at me.

"Are you okay?" she asks. "I was calling your name but you kind of zoned out. Well, I *was* calling you 'Bruce,' which isn't really your name, so it's no wonder you didn't respond. Sorry, this fake identity stuff is all new for me. In fact, this whole Meta thing is new to me. I don't think I'm going to be very good at it."

"Hey, don't say that," I say, shifting to face her. "I think you'll be great. I mean, you're the one who temporarily blinded Mr. Mister. And you came up with the plan to see the president. By the way, what's the name on your ticket anyway?"

"Diana Prince," she says, holding her ticket. "It's—"

"—Wonder Woman's secret identity," I finish for her. "Yeah, I know. I'm a big comic book fan."

"Me too," she says.

"See," I say. "Then you already know the deal. With great power comes—"

"—great responsibility," she finishes. "Yeah, I know. I just wish I was better at it. My parents don't think I'm good at anything."

"Really?" I say surprised.

"Yeah," she says, playing with her phone. "They're workaholics. I was pretty much raised by babysitters."

"Well, just think," I say. "You're better off than Tarzan. He was raised by apes. At least you got juice boxes."

She snorts and then shoots me a funny look.

"You're really good at this superhero stuff," she says. "I wish I could be as good as you."

"You will be," I say. "You just need proper training. Look, if I didn't have the Freedom Force, I wouldn't know half the stuff I'm doing. They taught me a lot."

"You're lucky," she says. "The three of us only have each other and we're all pretty new. If we don't have a Freedom Force to train us, how will we learn?"

That's a great question. I mean, I guess maybe I could train them. Maybe in the afternoon and...

Hang on, who am I kidding? I can't train these kids! I mean, I'm a lousy leader. And I'm not even allowed off the Waystation without my parents' permission.

Ugh. The Waystation. I feel sick.

I look over at Selfie who is spinning her phone around her finger. Then, I remember that's no normal phone. She used it to create a massive, blinding light. But as far as I'm aware, there's no app for that, so how did she do it?

"How does that thing work?" I whisper.

"This?" she whispers back, holding up her phone. "Well, honestly, I'm not really sure. I got it for my birthday but as soon as I held it, it sort of, well, spoke to me. I can make it do all sorts of things, depending on what I'm thinking, but I need to point the screen at whatever I'm using it against for it to work."

"It sounds like Magic," I say. "Like how Master Mime uses willpower to control his mystical amulet."

"Really?" she says. "I have powers like Master Mime? That's so cool. See, I'm already learning from you."

"Yeah," I say. "I guess so."

We gab about her powers for a while longer, when the bus finally SCREECHES to a halt. I look out the window, surprised to see we're parked at a bus stop, which means we've reached Washington D.C.

"Wow, that went fast," I say.

"Yeah," Selfie says, standing up. "Time to go."

"Great," I say. "Have fun without me."

"What?" she says confused. "Aren't you coming?"

"I'd love to," I say, "but a two-ton walrus is sleeping on my feet."

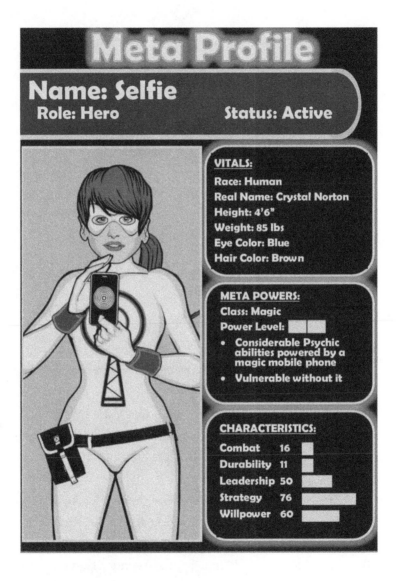

Meta Profile

Name: Selfie
Role: Hero
Status: Active

VITALS:

Race: Human
Real Name: Crystal Norton
Height: 4'6"
Weight: 85 lbs
Eye Color: Blue
Hair Color: Brown

META POWERS:

Class: Magic
Power Level:
- Considerable Psychic abilities powered by a magic mobile phone
- Vulnerable without it

CHARACTERISTICS:

Combat	16
Durability	11
Leadership	50
Strategy	76
Willpower	60

SEVEN

I TAKE A DETOUR OF THE WHITE HOUSE

I've never seen such a show of force.

The bus dropped us six blocks from the White House, and the closer we get, the more guards we encounter. At first, there were just police cars, but the last few blocks were packed with tanks and serious artillery. Not to mention the Meta-Busters stationed on every corner.

Fortunately, Dog-Gone is staying invisible, so we just look like four kids out for a morning stroll. But there's no way I can risk taking him into the White House with us. So, as soon as we hit Pennsylvania Avenue, I give him a stern talking to.

"Listen, Dog-Gone," I say. "It's important you stay

invisible and don't move from this spot. I don't care if a squirrel bops you on the head. Stay here until we get back. Got it?"

I feel a wet nose press into my palm.

"Good boy," I say. "Hopefully, we'll be back in an hour. Now remember, stay put."

Then, I nod to the others and we make our way to the White House gates.

"Do you think he'll listen?" Pinball asks.

"Oh, sure," I say. But deep down, I'm not so sure.

When we arrive there's a big crowd of senior citizens funneling through the entrance, so we fall in line behind them. Okay, all we need to do is get through security and we're home free. I just hope Selfie knows what she's doing.

But when I look up, I nearly have a heart attack.

"Um, big problem," I whisper to Selfie.

"What?" she says.

"They're making us walk through a metal detector," I say. "My utility belt will set that thing off like crazy."

"Don't worry about it," she says, moving forward.

Despite her confidence, my instincts tell me to turn and run, but just then, the last old lady waddles through the gate and it's our turn! I take a quick count of the guards. There's one in front collecting tickets, one monitoring the metal detector, and six lining the entry— and they're all holding machine guns.

Suddenly, my palms feel sweaty. I mean, if we get

caught, this will be a disaster. Especially after I spot a Meta-Buster standing in the wings.

"Tickets please," the guard requests. "And then step right through the metal detector."

"Sure," Selfie says. "But do you mind if I get a picture with all of you first? It's my first time here and I really want to capture the full experience."

"Sorry, dear," he says. "You can take all the pictures you want inside. I just need your ticket."

"Oh, please?" Selfie pleads. "Just one? It'll be quick. I just need everyone to lean in a bit."

The guard looks back at his colleagues and the guy behind the metal detector shrugs his shoulders.

"Okay," the guard says, rolling his eyes. "Just one."

"Great," she says. "Everyone look at my phone."

All of the guards scooch forward and smile as Selfie points her phone. I turn away before the big flash.

"Thanks," Selfie says. "Here's my ticket. And these guys are with me. You'll let us inside, right?"

"I'll let you inside," the guard repeats robotically like he's in some kind of a trance. And when I walk past, I notice his eyes are glazed over.

"Thanks," Selfie says. Then, she looks at the guard behind the metal detector and says, "Don't worry about our bags. It's all cool."

"It's all cool," the second guard repeats.

As we coast through without a hitch, I make a mental note: never photo bomb Selfie's pictures.

"See," Selfie says with a wink. "Told ya."

"Yes, you did," I say. "Nice job."

Once inside, we have no problem catching up with the other tourists who are ambling their way up the circular driveway. As we walk, I take it all in, amazed. I mean, I've probably seen the White House a million times on TV, but I've never actually been here.

That's when I notice a bespectacled woman heading our way who is wearing a big badge around her neck that reads: *Tour Guide.*

"Welcome to the White House," she says, with open arms. "My name is Lynn Douglas and it's my privilege to once again welcome the finalists from the forty-third Americana Quilting Contest." Then, she spots the four of us bringing up the rear. "Oh, and I see we have some young quilters this year. How wonderful. Please follow me."

"Quilting contest?" Pinball whispers. "No wonder we're surrounded by old people."

"Shhh!" Skunk Girl whispers. "Don't be rude."

"As you know," the tour guide continues, "the White House is the official residence and workplace of every president of the United States since John Adams, our second president, in the year 1800. This building has a fascinating history we'll discuss further inside. But before anyone asks, there are one hundred and thirty-two rooms and thirty-five bathrooms. Of course, we won't be seeing them all, but it's your lucky day because this tour received permission to visit the West Wing."

"The West Wing?" Selfie says. "That's amazing. That's where the Oval Office is located."

"Well, if the oval office is amazing," Pinball says, rubbing his round belly, "then I must be incredible."

"You don't get it, do you?" Skunk Girl says. "The Oval Office is the president's office."

The president's office? That's right! If this tour takes us straight to President Kensington's office, then I can discuss the Meta Restriction Resolution with her.

"Come this way," the tour guide says, ushering us into a long, covered pavilion that opens up to a beautiful garden. "We are walking through the West Colonnade, which connects the main residence to the West Wing. The West Colonnade overlooks the Rose Garden where many official events take place, including receptions and bill signings. Despite its name, you might be surprised to learn there are over thirty types of tulips in the Rose Garden. And to our left are—"

I'm sure what she's saying is fascinating, but the particulars of the Rose Garden are the last thing on my mind. If this tour is going to drop me at the president's doorstep, I need to figure out what I'm going to say!

I mean, how am I going to convince her to change her mind about Metas? Based on her last transmission, she seemed pretty dead set on stopping all Metas no matter what. Not even Dad could convince her otherwise, and he's freaking Captain Justice. So, what can

I possibly offer?

Suddenly, I realize we're inside another part of the building. This must be the West Wing, which means I'd better come up with something fast!

"To your left is the Cabinet Room," the tour guide continues. "Here is where the president seeks council from her top advisors. As you can imagine, many spirited debates are held around this twenty-foot table, like the recent ban on Metas."

"I want to break that table," Pinball whispers.

"Shhh!" Skunk Girl whispers, giving him a death stare.

The tour continues into another corridor filled with busy White House staffers. Some are running around carrying files while others are answering phone call after phone call. It's so chaotic I nearly miss seeing a door to our left that's flanked by two men in dark suits who look like Secret Service agents.

"Through that door is the Oval Office," the tour guide says. "But since the door is closed it looks like President Kensington is hard at work running the country. So, we won't have the opportunity to see it today, but there's still more ahead, like the Roosevelt Room. Follow me."

The crowd moans in disappointment, but as they move on, I can't help but linger.

"Hey," Selfie whispers, grabbing my arm. "Come on, you'll never get through. There are way too many people."

But just as she pulls me down the hall, I see a familiar face heading our way. I'd recognize those piercing, blue eyes anywhere. It's General Winch! And he's headed straight for the Oval Office!

Now's my chance!

I take in the scene. The staffers are busy doing their jobs, the tour is heading down the hall, and the Secret Service has their eyes on Winch. No one is looking my way. My heart is pounding fast. It's now or never.

Then, I remember I'm wearing my backpack. I can't risk my utility belt rattling around.

"Take this," I whisper to Selfie, handing her my backpack. But as I pass it over, something falls out of the top and hits the floor with a CLANG.

Great. I guess the bag wasn't zipped all the way.

"What's that?" Selfie says, bending over to pick it up.

"Doesn't matter," I whisper. "Just get ready."

"Get ready?" she whispers. "For what?"

But I don't have time to explain. Instead, I concentrate hard, reaching out for Dog-Gone's power. I extend my scope far and wide like a giant Meta Wi-Fi signal, pushing my power outside the building. I told that pooch to stay put. I just hope he listened.

Come on, Dog-Gone. Where are you? Please tell me you're not chasing some stupid squirrel.

And then, I connect!

Yes! He listened to me! I pull his power back until I

can feel it surging through my veins, and then I disappear.

"Hey," Selfie whispers. "Where'd you go?"

"I'm here," I whisper. "Create a distraction."

Suddenly, Selfie starts coughing.

All eyes turn to her.

Perfect!

Just then, Winch approaches the Oval Office. The Secret Service agents step aside and one of them opens the door. This is it! I've got to move!

But I also have to be careful. I may be invisible, but they could still hear me coming. So, I get on my tippy toes and fast-walk my way right behind Winch, matching him stride for stride. I'm so close I can smell his overpowering cologne. Gross!

"Gentlemen," Winch says, nodding to the agents.

I stay as close as I can without touching him, resisting the urge to pinch my nose as we both walk straight through the door. I can hear my heart thumping out of my chest. Please, heart, don't give me away.

And then the door miraculously SHUTS behind us.

Holy cow! I did it! I'm actually standing in the president's office! But then, Winch stops short and I nearly crash into him. Fortunately, I regain my balance just in time and take a quick look around.

We're standing on the edge of a plush, blue carpet with an image of the seal of the United States woven into its center. And it's pretty obvious how the Oval Office got its name because the room is shaped like, well, an oval. There are two cream-colored sofas behind us and paintings of former presidents line the walls.

It's swanky, but I'm not here to admire the décor. I'm here to have a word with the most powerful person on the planet—President Kara Kensington.

Despite our arrival, she's sitting quietly behind a large, mahogany desk with her eyes glued to a file. I'm sure she knows Winch is here, but clearly, she's not planning on acknowledging his presence. I still don't know what I'm going to say, but I guess you can't rehearse things like this. But just as I'm about to make myself visible, she looks up with steely eyes and says—

"I have no patience for idle pleasantries, General. Just give me the update."

"Certainly, my lord," Winch says.

Um, did he just call her 'my lord?' Isn't the whole point of a democracy not to have Kings or Queens?

"We have apprehended three more superhero teams," Winch says proudly. "The Storm Squad, the Watchdogs, and the Marvelous Monsters. The last one resulted in several hundred casualties."

"To be expected," President Kensington says matter-of-factly, closing her file. "It is a small price to pay."

"Yes, my lord," Winch says. "The surviving prisoners have all been transferred to the Pentagon to begin behavior modification and the leeching process."

Leeching process? What's that?

"Excellent," she says. "And the hatchlings?"

"The bio-engineering lab has produced thirty-one more," Winch says. Then, he swallows hard and adds, "but we have lost forty-five due to contamination."

"Unacceptable!" President Kensington yells, pounding her desk.

That's when I notice the surface of her desk is actually cracked like she's done this before.

"Has the root cause of the contamination been identified yet?" she asks.

"No, my lord," Winch says. "The scientists believe it has something to do with the levels of nitrogen in the atmosphere. They are depressurizing the line and—"

"Enough!" she barks. "Please inform them that if this issue is not resolved by tomorrow morning, the only thing that will be depressurized is their hides."

"Yes, my lord," Winch says.

Okay, at this point, I'm thinking I made a huge mistake. I mean, if the president of the United States is acting like a tyrant and making people call her 'my lord,' then there's no way little old me is going to convince her to change her tune about the Meta Restriction Resolution.

I think it's time I made my exit.

I take one step backward when I hear—

"And the Orb Master?" President Kensington asks.

I freeze. Did she just say, 'Orb Master?'

No one's called me that in like, forever.

"He… escaped," Winch says.

"Escaped?" she says. "And what are we doing to find

him? Our plan is dependent on him."

"My Meta-Busters are searching for him now," Winch says. "We will not let him escape our grasp."

"You seem to forget yourself, General," she says. "For *your* Meta-Busters are, in fact, *my* Meta-Busters."

"Of course, my lord," Winch says. "A mere slip of the tongue. As long as I am programming them, they serve at your disposal."

"Indeed," President Kensington says. "But it does not excuse the fact that the Orb Master has escaped your robots. Perhaps I..."

Huh? Why'd she stop talking?

And why is she looking down at my feet?

Then, I glance down and my stomach sinks.

Because right where I was standing is an imprint of my foot on the plush carpet. I'm such a fool. I may be invisible, but I'm not weightless!

"Guards!" she commands. "Infrared!"

Uh-oh. Before I can move, two Meta-Busters emerge out of nowhere, their eyes flickering red.

"Seize him!" she yells.

I make a break for the door when I'm suddenly engulfed in a thick, green mist. It smells like rotten eggs, but I've got to keep moving. I've got to get out of here!

But as I reach for the door, the room starts spinning!

My hand misses the doorknob by a mile and I suddenly hit the floor hard.

I try pushing myself up, but I can't move a muscle.

My eyelids are getting heavy.

I just need… to… focus.

But… I can't… keep my eyes… open.

And then, everything goes dark.

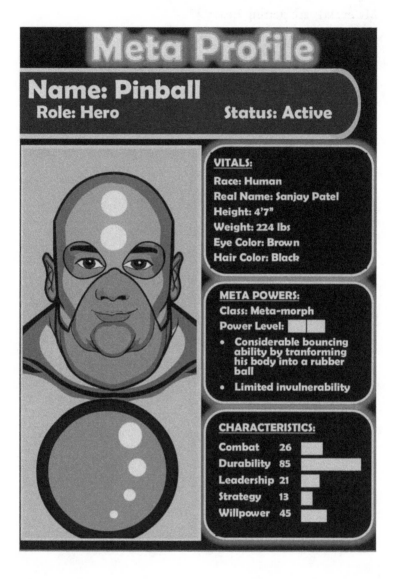

Meta Profile

Name: Pinball
Role: Hero   Status: Active

VITALS:

Race: Human
Real Name: Sanjay Patel
Height: 4'7"
Weight: 224 lbs
Eye Color: Brown
Hair Color: Black

META POWERS:

Class: Meta-morph
Power Level:
- Considerable bouncing ability by tranforming his body into a rubber ball
- Limited invulnerability

CHARACTERISTICS:

Combat	26	
Durability	85	
Leadership	21	
Strategy	13	
Willpower	45	

EIGHT

I NEED A PRESIDENTIAL PARDON

I open my eyes only to wish I hadn't.

I'm in a dark, dingy, concrete room no bigger than an ambulance. The door is bolted shut, and there's a narrow window high on the opposite wall that doesn't look like it opens to the outside. My first instinct is to get out of here, but when I try to move, I'm stuck. That's when I realize my arms and legs are tied to metal posts!

This is not good.

And the room smells like rotten cheese, which may be worse.

"Welcome back to the land of the living," echoes a woman's voice that startles me.

"Who's there?" I ask, my eyes darting all over the place. But there's no one there.

"Don't you remember me?" the woman says, stepping out of the shadows.

"President Kensington!" I say, my eyes going wide.

What's she doing here?

But then it all comes flooding back: the Meta Restriction Resolution. The Meta-Busters. My family.

"Let me go!" I yell.

"You're in no position to be making demands," she says. "None at all."

"Where am I?" I ask.

"In one of the secret sub-basements of this pitiful hovel you call the White House," she says. "It is quite a dump for the supposed leader of the free world. Truthfully, I had expected so much more from your species, but I suppose I have become conditioned to these frequent disappointments."

'Your species?' What's she talking about?

And then I remember she called me 'Orb Master.'

No one from Earth ever calls me 'Orb Master.'

And that's when a chill runs down my spine.

"Who-Who are you?" I ask, fearing the answer.

Then, I watch in horror as her body morphs from the diminutive shape of President Kara Kensington into a towering figure with big muscles and pointy ears.

My jaw hits the floor.

Because she was never President Kensington at all!

In fact, she's not even a she.

It's… it's…

"Bow before your king," the Skelton Emperor says, smiling with glee.

"W-Where's the real president?" I blurt out.

"Let us just say she is my honored guest," the Emperor says. "Along with dignitaries from across the globe."

Across the globe?

"Wait," I say. "Are you telling me those other world leaders are Skelton phonies too?"

"Not phonies," he says, waving his finger. "Skelton operatives. We have taken over your planet by replacing your leaders one by one. It was not difficult. In fact, we assumed complete control of your civilization well ahead of schedule. And your fellow humans are still none the wiser."

Um, what?

He's telling me the Skelton have taken over Earth!

And I'm the only one who knows it!

"B-But I don't get it," I say. "What are you even doing here? What do you want?"

"That is simple," he says. "Earth will become the hub of the Skelton Empire—the new Skelton Homeworld. And all Earthlings will become my servants."

The new Skelton Homeworld?

But that doesn't make sense.

The Skelton already have a—

Suddenly, I remember my conversation with Wind

Walker. It was right after our adventure in the 13th Dimension. I was so happy to see him that I didn't think much about it at the time, but he told me the Skelton Homeworld had been taken over by... by...

"Krule the Conqueror!" I blurt out. "You lost your world to Krule the Conqueror, and now you've scampered here with your tail between your legs to take over mine!"

"Silence, child!" the Emperor yells. "You are in the presence of royalty, and royalty never 'scampers.' Besides, you may believe Earth is rightfully yours, but the truth is, we've been inhabiting this planet for far longer than your kind. Earth is as much mine as it is yours."

"What?" I say confused.

"Oh, yes," he says. "It may be hard to believe, but we had identified Earth as a viable backup homeworld long before humans came into existence. Our scouts have been monitoring your planet for hundreds of centuries, operating as silent observers by blending into the background. If we ever needed to colonize your world, we knew we could easily dominate your kind. But over the last fifty years, new threats started to emerge. A growing sub-population of Earthlings began exhibiting strange new abilities—Meta abilities—and we could not risk this development upsetting our plans."

My jaw is hanging open. I mean, based on what he's saying, Skelton agents have been hiding here in plain sight for, well, forever! Is he serious?

But then I remember K'ami. She could morph into an ordinary housefly. And she told me that flies made their way to the Skelton Homeworld thousands of years ago as stowaways on scout ships that had visited Earth.

So, I guess what he's saying must be true!

It's no wonder the world has flipped out on Metas.

All of our world leaders are Skelton!

"But there's one thing I don't understand," I say. "Why did Krule even attack your planet in the first place? What's he got against you?"

"That is none of your concern," the Emperor says, raising his chin.

"I disagree," I shoot back. "Because if you're here, Krule's gonna follow you here too. And if an entire planet of Skelton couldn't stop him, what makes you think you're going to stop him here?"

"That is simple," he says, "Because here on Earth lives the most powerful weapon in the universe."

"Aaannnd, what's that?" I ask, my eyebrows raised.

"You," he says.

For some reason, I knew it.

That's probably why those Meta-Busters were trying to capture me alive—at least at first. But if he's thinking I'm the most powerful weapon in the universe, he probably thinks I have the Orb of Oblivion. So, now's my chance to rain on his insane parade.

"Sorry to interrupt this ill-conceived scheme," I say, "but here's a newsflash for you. I don't have the Orb of

Oblivion anymore, so I guess you can leave."

There. That should do it.

"Oh, don't worry," he says. "My plan does not require the Orb of Oblivion."

"Um, what?" I say shocked. "I don't get it?"

"Don't you?" the Emperor says. "Amongst all Metas in the known universe, your power is rare. There are but a few Metas who can manipulate Meta energy. And one of them is heading here."

"Hold up," I say. "I've seen this movie before and I'm not going back for the sequel. If you think I'm taking on Krule the Conqueror, then you're even nuttier than I remember."

Okay, I've got to get out of here. I may not have the Orb of Oblivion, but I do have my powers. And since the Emperor is a Skelton, it should be a snap to borrow his.

I concentrate hard, ready to push out my energy.

But I feel… nothing?

That's weird. Maybe I'm tired. I focus and reach out again, but I still don't feel anything.

Suddenly, the Emperor laughs.

"Fool," he says. "Did you think I would risk my own safety in your presence? Clearly, you do not recognize the organisms restraining you?"

Organisms?

I glance up at my left arm to find a leathery, brown material wrapped around my wrist. Holy cow! That's the stuff I've been trying to identify. It's thick, with a rippled hide. I know I've seen it before.

But what could it—

And then it hits me.

I have seen this organism before, but never like this! In fact, the last time I laid hands on one was when K'ami was alive and we were facing the High Commander inside of Lockdown. That didn't end so well either.

"Sheelds?" I say. "You're using Sheelds to dampen Meta powers? But I didn't think they could do that."

"You are correct," the Emperor says, grinning. "Typical Sheelds cannot do that. Due to their unique genetic makeup, Sheelds are the only creatures in the universe who can resist all forms of external stimulation. Fortunately, I am not harvesting typical Sheelds."

"Harvesting?" I say. "What are you talking about?"

"I am talking about genetic engineering," he says. "My scientists are growing a new type of Sheeld right here on Earth. One whose abilities are not wasted on itself but can be transferred to others through physical contact."

Physical contact?

Suddenly, everything makes perfect sense.

That's why Blue Bolt, Makeshift, and Master Mime couldn't fight back! That's why my parents became helpless and got captured! That's why my powers aren't working now!

The Skelton are using these 'super-Sheelds' to suppress Meta powers. As long as these creatures are touching me, I'm powerless!

"But that is not all," he continues. "The harvesting process requires something your planet has in spades."

"And what's that?" I ask.

"Meta energy," the Emperor says. "The process of converting a Sheeld requires an abundance of Meta energy. That is why the heroes of your world are so valuable."

Wait, what? He's using Meta energy to create these super-Sheelds? So, is that what this Meta Restriction Resolution is really about? Is that why he's collecting Meta heroes—to steal their Meta energy?

But if that's the case, there's still something I don't understand.

"If you want Meta energy," I say, "then why are you only focused on capturing Meta heroes? What about all of those Meta villains out there? Why aren't your Meta-Busters going after those guys?"

"Because villains care about nothing but themselves," he answers matter-of-factly.

"Yeah?" I say. "So?"

"So," he repeats, "that makes them much harder to capture. Do you know what makes heroes so vulnerable?"

"Um, not really," I say.

"Self-sacrifice," the Emperor says. "Heroes will risk everything for the welfare of others. Therefore, they are far easier to manipulate. So, until I run out of heroes, I do not have to bother chasing villains."

Wow, I hate to admit it, but he's got a point there. I

mean, my parents dropped everything to save our friends.

But they also flew right into his trap.

"Look," I say. "I don't know what you're expecting me to do, but I'm not going to help you."

"That is where you are wrong," he says. "After all, you too are a hero. Could you really just stand back and watch Krule the Conqueror take over your world?"

Well, he's got me there.

"You will act as my champion," the Emperor continues. "You will use your powers to defeat Krule the Conqueror and save your planet. But first, you must be properly trained."

"Trained?" I say. "Look, I know how to fight. And by the way, I've saved this freaking planet a few times already, including from your kind. Besides, I never agreed to do this. Why would I fight Krule just to leave Earth to you?"

"I thought you might resist," he says, moving towards the door. "So, I brought some added motivation." Then, he swings the door open.

The next thing I know, General Winch enters, pushing a brown-haired girl in front of him. Her head is down and her wrists are bound by a super-Sheeld.

Then, the Emperor lifts her face, and my heart sinks.

"Selfie!" I call out.

She looks at me with terror in her eyes.

"I thought you might recognize her," the Emperor says. "And do not worry, I have your other friends as well. They put up a good fight for ones so young, but in the end, they were no match for my Blood Bringers."

I feel sick to my stomach.

I knew I shouldn't have brought them here.

"Release her!" I demand.

"Now why would I do that?" he says. "You will help me defeat Krule, or your friends will die, starting with this one. Is that motivating enough for you?"

I want to yell out in frustration, but it's no use.

He's got me.

And there's nothing I can do about it.

Reluctantly, I nod in agreement.

"Excellent," the Emperor says. "I suggest you get some rest because the next time we meet I will train you in the Skelton Code of Combat. And then we will see if you have what it takes to survive."

NINE

I STINK AT TESTS

It feels like I've been trapped in this room forever.

My arms have been stuck to these posts for so long it feels like they're gonna fall off. And I can't tell if it's day or night because that little window looks like it goes to another interior room. But who am I to complain? This is probably a fitting punishment for all of the mistakes I've made.

Truthfully, I've resigned myself to my fate anyway. The super-Sheelds have neutralized my powers, and I'm not strong enough to break free on my own. So, I guess all I can look forward to is another visit from the Emperor.

Now that's depressing.

The last time I saw him, he told me he'd be back to

train me in the Skelton Code of Combat, whatever that is.

He just never told me when.

Needless to say, I've had plenty of time to torture myself about all of the bad decisions I've made.

Over and over and over again.

I mean, I never should have called Dad from the Waystation, I never should have brought Next Gen to the White House, and I never should have assumed the president was who she appeared to be.

Some hero I turned out to be.

A tear runs down my cheek but I can't even wipe it away. Who knows what's happened to my family? And poor Dog-Gone is probably lost in Washington D.C.

I'm the worst hero to ever put on a mask. Not that I'm even wearing a mask right now.

But despite how crummy I feel, I know I've got to shake it off. Wallowing in self-pity isn't going to get me out of this mess. I need a plan to bust out of here.

The question is how?

BOOM!

Suddenly, the door bursts open and my heart skips a hopeful beat. But instead of the cavalry, it's Winch!

"The time has come," he says, his blue eyes narrowing.

"Um, you sure about that?" I say. "Because I'm good just hanging out here."

But Winch ignores me and unties my left arm from the post. For a split second, I have grandiose visions of a great escape, but as soon as my appendage falls limply to my side, I realize I have no sensation in my arm, and Winch easily re-wraps the super-Sheeld around my wrist. Well, so much for riding off into the sunset. A few minutes later, I'm free from the posts but still wearing my super-Sheeld restraints.

Then, Winch grabs my shirt collar.

"Easy," I say. "These aren't my threads."

My legs feel like jelly as Winch pulls me out of the room, but he doesn't seem to care. Instead, he yanks me through a series of creepy corridors. I have no idea where we are, but I'm pretty sure none of this is on the official White House tour.

He leads me down a steep flight of stairs into a room bigger than a football field—and standing in the center is the Skelton Emperor.

His arms are crossed and his eyes never leave mine as Winch drags me over to meet him. All I want is to slap that big smirk off of his face, but that's not going to get me anywhere. At least not yet.

"Report," the Emperor barks.

"Our scouts have detected Krule's armada entering the Alpha Centauri solar system," Winch says. "Based on his current coordinates, we expect him to enter Earth's atmosphere in fourteen point three days."

"Very good," the Emperor says. "Wait outside."

"Yes, my lord," Winch says, with a bow. Then, he exits, leaving me all alone with the Emperor.

"As you just heard," the Emperor says, "time is of the essence. For you to be victorious in your fight with Krule, you will need to reprogram your weak hero mindset. You must learn to fight like a Skelton: ruthless, cunning, and savage. If you fail to embrace what I teach you, you will perish."

"Sounds awesome," I say. "But just so you know, I'm not great at taking tests. So, if there's like, a pop quiz at the end of this you can just give me an 'F' now."

"Silence!" he barks, his foul breath hitting my nostrils. "You will speak only upon command. Is that understood?"

I nod, not giving him the satisfaction of hearing my answer.

"I asked you a question," the Emperor says. "I expect a verbal answer."

We stare each other down. But then I realize if I'm going to win the war, I may need to lose a few battles.

"Yes," I say reluctantly.

"Excellent," he says, towering over me. "Now you will learn the Skelton Code of Combat. It is more than a battle plan; it is a warrior philosophy designed to give you the upper hand in defeating any enemy. Shall we begin?"

"Sure," I say. Based on his serious expression I feel like I should be taking notes or something.

"Principle number one," he says. "Never show weakness."

Wait? Never show weakness?

That's what K'ami used to say to me. At first, I think it's just a funny coincidence, but then I remember she was a Skelton too. She must have gotten it from the Skelton Code of Combat!

"Principle number two," the Emperor continues. "Always go on the offensive. Principle number three: Use the element of surprise. And finally, principle number four: Show no mercy. These are the four principles that make up the Skelton Code of Combat. These are the principles ingrained in the minds of Skelton Blood Bringers from birth. These are the principles you must learn now."

"Got it," I say. "But I'm more than happy to wait on the whole Krule showdown thing. I mean, I'd still like to get my driver's license one day and—"

"Silence!" the Emperor bellows, his voice echoing through the room. "You will speak only when requested. Now, repeat the Skelton Code of Combat."

"Never show weakness," I say proudly.

The Emperor nods.

See, I was listening. Now for the other three.

Um, what were the other three again? I was so busy thinking about K'ami I missed what he said.

"Repeat," the Emperor commands.

"Hold your horses," I say, trying to remember. "Okay. The second was to be offensive. The third was something about using the element of French fries. And the last one was... What was that last one again?"

But the Emperor doesn't answer me. Instead, he looks like he wants to murder me.

"Let me try again," I say. "I'll nail it this time. Promise."

"If you do not take these lessons seriously," he says, "you will lose. Krule is a killer, and he will dispose of you with the mere blink of his third eye."

"Gee, thanks for the pep talk," I say. "You know, maybe teaching isn't the right career field for you. Maybe you should stick to the stuff you're good at, like ruining people's lives and being generally annoying."

"Enough!" he says. "I have tried to provide you with the tools for victory, but clearly you believe you do not need them. Very well then, let us put your skills to the test."

Okay, now we're talking. I'll do anything to stop his jowls from flapping.

The next thing I know, the Emperor reaches down and removes the super-Sheelds from my wrists and ankles. Well, I wasn't expecting that. And for a moment, I consider using my duplication powers to take him out. But then I remember he's still holding Selfie and the others captive. I don't know where they are and I can't risk anything happening to them, so I'll have to make my move at another time.

"Prepare yourself, child," he says, flashing a strange smile. "Because your enemy is here. Prepare to fight Krule the Conqueror!"

Wait, what?

I spin around and my whole body goes numb because standing on the other side of the room is a giant, red-skinned man with three eyes.

It's... Krule!

But what's he doing here? Didn't Winch just say he's weeks away from Earth? How'd he get here so fast?

"Good luck," the Emperor says.

"H-Hang on a minute," I stammer, backing up.

My heart is beating a mile a minute and my brain freezes up. What should I do? I wasn't ready for this!

"Principle number one," the Emperor says, snapping me back to reality. "Never show weakness."

OMG! He's right. The way I'm fumbling around has got to be giving Krule more confidence. I probably look like I'm going to pass out. I need to get a hold of myself. I may not feel brave, but at least I can look brave.

I stop in my tracks and stare Krule down.

Then, Krule's third eye radiates with green energy.

Uh-oh. Maybe I was better off fumbling.

Suddenly, there's incredible pressure in my brain! It's like he's got my head in a vice and he's trying to crush it!

The pain is so intense I drop to my knees.

"Principle number two," comes the Emperor's faint voice. "Always go on the offensive."

G-Go... on the offensive? Yeah. G-Great idea, if I could concentrate. B-But if I don't act now, I'm dead meat.

Come on, Elliott! Focus!

I grit my teeth and gather all of the negation power I can muster, and then I lash out in Krule's direction. My brain is so on fire I can't even look up. I'm just praying I made contact.

Suddenly, the pressure stops.

Yes, I did it!

I rise unsteadily to my feet and face my opponent. Shockingly, Krule hasn't moved from his spot. In fact, he seems content to simply destroy me from a distance. I don't think I've ever faced a Psychic with this kind of raw power before. Even the Shadow from the 13th Dimension pales in comparison.

I've got to strike while he's out of—

Just then, his third eye lights up again.

—power?

Suddenly, I'm blown off my feet and slam into the concrete wall behind me. My back hits hard, and the next thing I know I'm on my hands and knees, wheezing for air.

This isn't going well.

"Principle number three," the Emperor says. "Use the element of surprise."

The element of surprise? That might work for your average alien mega-menace, but how the heck do you surprise Krule the Conqueror?

I look around for something to use, but the room is empty, except for Krule and… the Emperor!

That's it. I've got a plan.

I cast my duplication powers at Krule and pull them back. There's a massive surge of energy dancing through my veins. But I can't just stand here admiring his power levels. I need to use them to create the element of surprise.

And the Emperor is perfect for that!

"What's happening?" the Emperor says, as I mentally lift his body off the ground using Krule's telekinesis. "Put me down at once!"

But I don't listen. Instead, I turn his flailing body horizontal, and then I launch him straight at Krule like a runaway missile. The Emperor SLAMS into Krule crown-first and they tumble to the ground, the Emperor lying flat on top of Krule.

Yes! Krule wasn't expecting that!

Now is my chance!

But as I hustle over to end the fight and save the universe, my jaw drops. Because when the Emperor rolls off of Krule's body, Krule is nowhere to be found, and in his place is the unconscious body of a girl with dark hair and a white mask with a teardrop painted under her right eye!

OMG! I know her.

It's Zen from the Rising Suns!

What's she doing here? But then I realize she's not moving! Is she...?

I kneel and check her pulse. Whew, she's still

breathing. But what's going on? And what happened to Krule?

And then it hits me.

Krule was never here at all.

This was just a test.

After all, Zen is a powerful Psychic in her own right, and the Emperor must have made her use her powers to trick me into believing I was facing Krule. But in reality, I was fighting Zen the whole time!

But why would Zen do that?

And then I feel a knot in my stomach.

This must be what 'behavior modification' means.

The Emperor must have brainwashed her.

"Well done, child," the Emperor says, getting to his feet and dusting off his armor. "You certainly used the element of surprise to great effect, although the next time you employ me as a projectile it will be the last thing you ever do. Now it is time to implement principle number four. Show no mercy. Finish the girl."

What?

"No way," I say. "I can't do that."

"If you are going to defeat Krule," he says, "you must kill him when you have the chance."

I stare at Zen's face.

She looks so young. So innocent.

"Kill her!" the Emperor demands. "End her life, or Krule will end yours."

"Sorry," I say, sitting down next to Zen. "I guess

that's just what Krule will have to do."

"Fool!" the Emperor yells. "You will die at his hand. You will—"

But he's just background noise because I've already tuned him out. I drop my head into my hands. Boy, I've really stepped in it this time. I have no idea how to get out of this mess. In fact, I'm not sure there's even a way out of this mess.

Suddenly, Winch appears and slaps a pair of super-Sheelds around my wrists. Then, he picks me up from beneath my armpits and carries me out of the room.

I try to stay alert, but I'm so mentally exhausted I can't keep my eyes open.

My eyelids feel so darn heavy.

"... pay for this...," I hear Winch grumble as he carries me upstairs, but I can't really make out what he's saying.

And then everything goes dark.

Meta Profile

Name: Zen
Role: Hero   Status: Active

VITALS:
Race: Human
Real Name: Mei Nakamura
Height: 4'3"
Weight: 78 lbs
Eye Color: Brown
Hair Color: Black

META POWERS:
Class: Psychic
Power Level:
- Extreme Telepathy
- Extreme Telekinesis
- Group Mind-Linking

CHARACTERISTICS:
Combat	35	
Durability	22	
Leadership	74	
Strategy	90	
Willpower	95	

TEN

I RUN INTO SOME OLD FRIENDS

I wake up in a fog.

My vision is cloudy and I attempt to wipe my eyes clear, but I can't move my arms. What gives? That's when I realize I'm back in my dingy cell. I must have passed out from exhaustion when Winch carried me up the stairs.

I squeeze my eyes tight and then open them again to clear up the cloudiness. Boy, I'd give anything to bust out of here, but with these super-Sheelds restraining me, I couldn't use my powers even if I tried. And it's not like anyone can hear me if I call for help.

Wait a minute. Call... for help?

Wind Walker!

He's rescued me before in situations like this. Like the time the Rising Suns held me prisoner in Japan. I'm such a dufus. Why didn't I think of him earlier?

Fortunately, I'm all alone and the door is closed. So, I take a deep breath and yell, "Wind Walker!"

But he doesn't show up.

Okay, don't panic. Maybe my voice isn't carrying since I'm buried in a concrete sub-basement who knows how many levels below the White House. This time I take a deeper breath and yell Wind Walker's name at the top of my lungs.

But he still doesn't show.

Okay, that's not good. The last time this happened he was trapped in the 13th Dimension. So, either he's in trouble again or these super-Sheelds are blocking our connection. Which basically means I'm stuck.

Fantabulous.

Suddenly, my stomach grumbles. The last thing I remember eating was a granola bar back at Next Gen's treehouse. If I don't eat something soon, I'll probably waste away before I even face Krule.

Hmmm, that might be a good thing.

Who am I kidding? There's no easy way out of this. After all, the Emperor is still holding Next Gen and my family captive. The only shot I have at saving them is to defeat Krule. And if I somehow survive that, then I'll have to deal with the Emperor and his Skelton henchmen.

Sounds like a piece of cake.

Not.

Honestly, I don't think I've ever faced a challenge this big before. Yeah, there was the Worm, and Meta-Taker, and Ravager, but it always seemed like there was a clear path to follow. This time, I don't see one.

I sure wish my parents were here. They'd know what to do. Even Grace would probably know what to do. But me, I'm clueless. Then, I get a scary thought. What if my family isn't my family anymore?

What if they're brainwashed?

I mean, if the Emperor could brainwash a Psychic as powerful as Zen, then what's he done with Mom and Dad? Mom is as powerful as Zen, and Dad is as strong-willed as they come. Are they the Emperor's mindless minions now?

If the answer is yes, then it really is all up to me.

I hang my head in defeat.

This is hopeless.

BOOM!

Suddenly, the door flies off its hinges!

I jolt up, fully expecting to see the Emperor standing in the doorframe, but instead, I'm staring at a slightly overweight German Shephard wagging his tail.

"Dog-Gone?"

I close my eyes, thinking I'm hallucinating, but when I open them again, Dog-Gone is still standing there. And now he's looking down the hall and pointing his nose at me like he's signaling to someone else.

Just then, two costumed characters burst into the

room. The guy has red-skin, blue goggles, and a large tail. And the girl is really tall, with blue markings on her face and two swords at her hips.

OMG! I can't believe it! It's—

"Scorpio? Taurus? What are you doing here?"

"Rescuing you," Taurus says. "Now stay still while Scorpio blasts the restraints."

All of a sudden, Scorpio's long tail sweeps past my face and hovers in front of my left wrist. Then, the tip turns bright orange and emits a precise beam of energy that pierces the first super-Sheeld. Instantly, the creature recoils, releasing my arm as it drops to the floor squirming.

Scorpio quickly attends to the other super-Sheelds, and as the last one falls, I flop into Taurus' arms like a ragdoll.

"Thanks," I say. "But how'd you know I was here?"

"We'll explain later," she says. "Because we're not out of the woods yet. Can you run?"

I want to say yes, but when I try to stand up, I feel woozy and collapse back into her arms.

"I'll take that as a 'no,'" she says, hoisting me over her shoulder. "Scorpio, let's go."

Believe me, I want nothing more than to get out of here, but then I remember something important.

"Wait!" I say. "We can't just leave. I have friends here who are prisoners of—"

"Don't worry," Taurus says, "the others got them."

The others? Like, Gemini? Is she here?

But I don't have time to ask Taurus the question because we're already on the move. I can't see much slung over Taurus' shoulder, except for Dog-Gone who is trailing behind, looking at me with concern in his eyes.

"D-Don't worry," I mutter. "I-I'm okay."

But the truth is, I'm far from okay. In fact, I don't think I've ever felt so feeble. Plus, I've got no clue how we're going to get out of here. I mean, the place is swarming with—

"Robots!" Scorpio yells.

THOOM!

There's a massive explosion. I wince as Taurus turns her back, shielding me from a hailstorm of debris. The Meta-Busters! They're right behind us! My heart is pumping fast. Even if I had the strength to help out, my powers are useless against robots.

THOOM!

YIP!

Dog-Gone!

I peer over Taurus' shoulder but I don't see him!

"We need another way out!" Taurus yells.

"Now!" Scorpio calls out.

RIIPPPP!

Suddenly, there's an ear-splitting noise and when I look up, the ceiling is gone! Through the falling debris, I think I spot something that looks like a silver submarine descending from the sky.

But then something hits the side of my head.

Ouch! My… temple…

And everything starts spinning...

***

"Serpentarius?"

I hear a faint voice. A girl's voice.

Familiar. But why?

"Epic Zero, are you okay?"

Huh? That's another girl's voice. A different girl.

What the heck happened and where am I?

I try opening my eyes but it feels like my eyelids are pinned down by toothpicks. It takes everything I've got, but eventually I manage to pry them open. That's when I realize I'm no longer in my cell. Instead, I'm lying on a table staring at a familiar-looking ceiling crisscrossed with wires.

It's the Ghost Ship!

I see Selfie on my left and smile. Thank goodness she's okay. I couldn't forgive myself if anything happened to her. But when I look to my right, I do a double take, because standing there is a pretty girl with green skin, orange eyes, and two antenna stalks poking through her long, black hair.

"G-Gemini?" I stammer. "Is that really you?"

"In the flesh," she says, putting her hand on my arm.

I can't believe it. The last time I saw Gemini was

when the Zodiac saved me before Arena World blew up into a gazillion pieces. And when we parted ways, she sort of, well, kissed me on the cheek.

"How do you feel?" Gemini asks. "Taurus said a piece of concrete hit you on your head."

"I'm okay," I say, but as soon as I touch my right temple, I feel a bandage, followed by shooting pain. "Then again, maybe not."

"I patched you up and gave you some medicine," Gemini says. "The pain should lesson soon."

"Gee, thanks," I say, shuffling up onto my elbows. "That was nice of you."

But when I look over at Selfie, she's looking cross-eyed at Gemini. Um, okay. Why is Selfie so upset?

"I wasn't sure I'd ever see you again," Gemini says, looking down. "I was glad you finally called."

"What?" I say. "But I didn't call."

"Apparently, I did," Selfie says, holding up a shiny object shaped like a serpent. "This trinket fell out of your backpack when you handed it to me. I didn't realize it, but I must have activated it when I picked it up."

OMG! That's my official Zodiac communications link! Pisces handed it to me before Wind Walker took me home. There was so much going on I completely forgot about it.

"Serpentarius!" comes another familiar voice.

I turn to find a short girl with spikey hair and gill-like flaps on her neck running towards me. And behind her is a bearded kid who looks half-human and half-horse.

It's Pisces and Sagittarius!

"It's great to see you, Serpentarius," Pisces says, hugging me.

"Serpentarius?" Selfie says confused. "I thought your superhero name was Epic Zero?"

"It is," I say. "Well, I mean, they both are. But Serpentarius is the name the Zodiac gave me when they made me an honorary member of their team. It's the thirteenth sign of the Zodiac."

"Wait a second," Selfie says, "you mean to tell me you joined their team, but not ours?"

"Um," I babble. "Well..."

"See?" Skunk Girl says, appearing behind her. "I told you we didn't need him."

"Yeah," Pinball says. "I guess you're right."

Boy, it's great those guys are safe too, even though they're clearly not so happy to see me.

"Serpentarius," Gemini says. "We never did get to thank you for defeating Ravager. On behalf of all of the members of the Zodiac, past, and present, we thank you for destroying that monster and avenging our worlds. You are truly the bravest hero in the multiverse."

"Um, thanks," I say, blushing. But I sure don't feel like the bravest hero in the multiverse. In fact, I'm pretty sure if they saw me cowering in front of Krule they'd be calling me something else.

Speaking of cowering...

"Hey, where is Dog-Gone?" I ask.

But no one answers me.

And when I look at their faces, no one looks back.

Instead, they're all looking down at their shoes.

"C'mon, guys," I say, laughing nervously. "Enough joking around. He's probably here somewhere just being his annoying, invisible self. Right?"

"I'm sorry, Serpentarius," Scorpio says, coming in from the bridge. "After we escaped, most of the building was completely obliterated. We circled back twice to look for him. We even used our infrared scanners. But we couldn't find him."

Suddenly, it feels like I've been kicked in the gut.

I open my mouth to speak, but nothing comes out.

"He was a brave and loyal companion," Taurus says, appearing behind Scorpio. "When we first arrived, he flagged us down immediately and used his keen sense of smell to lead us straight to your friends, and ultimately, to you. You should be proud of him. He died an honorable death."

The words strike me oddly.

Dog-Gone. Died?

An... honorable death?

Others give their condolences, but I don't hear them.

Instead, all I see is Dog-Gone's face. All I think about are the millions of crazy adventures we've had together. The arguments over dog treats. The belly rubs. The slobbery hugs.

But now… he's gone.

And so is the Waystation.

And who knows what's happened to my parents?

Or Grace.

Or the Freedom Force.

And it's all because of two people.

The Emperor and Krule the freaking Conqueror.

"Epic Zero?" Selfie says. "Are you okay?"

Okay? No, I'm not okay. I'm… numb.

But that feeling is quickly replaced by another. A feeling building inside of me that I can't control.

A feeling of rage.

"Epic Zero?" Selfie repeats.

"I'm fine," I say, matter-of-factly. Then, I rip the bandage off my head and stand up. "It's time."

"Time?" Gemini repeats. "For what?"

"Revenge," I say. "But first I need to call a friend."

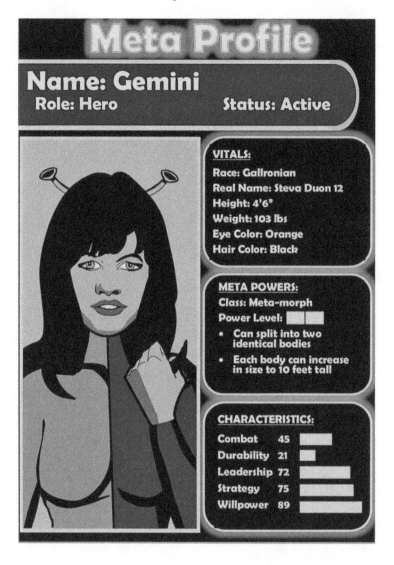

Meta Profile

Name: Gemini
Role: Hero   Status: Active

VITALS:

Race: Gallronian
Real Name: Steva Duon 12
Height: 4'6"
Weight: 103 lbs
Eye Color: Orange
Hair Color: Black

META POWERS:

Class: Meta-morph
Power Level:
- Can split into two identical bodies
- Each body can increase in size to 10 feet tall

CHARACTERISTICS:

Combat	45	
Durability	21	
Leadership	72	
Strategy	75	
Willpower	89	

ELEVEN

I UNCOVER MORE PROBLEMS

I'm holding on with everything I've got.

There's a strong force pushing against us and my cheeks are literally blowing backward, but I can't let go, otherwise, I'm pretty sure I'll be lost forever. So, I squeeze even tighter and hang on for dear life. But just when I think I can't hold on any longer, there's a loud POP and I tumble out the other side.

When I finally stop rolling, I see my old friend standing over me with a big smile on his blue face.

"I thought you would be used to it by now," Wind Walker says, extending a hand.

"Clearly not," I say, taking his hand and getting to my feet. "I'm not sure how anyone could get used to traveling by wormhole, including you. But getting inside this place would have been impossible without your help."

"Indeed," Wind Walker says. "I have never seen a facility so well guarded before. What is the name of this place again?"

"The Pentagon," I say.

"Yes," he says. "I am glad my powers allowed us to slip through their defenses undetected."

He's right about that. With all of the Meta-Busters circling, there was no way I'd get within half a mile of here without Wind Walker's help. I'm just glad he answered my call this time.

"I still do not understand why I did not hear you the first time," Wind Walker says. "I was not in any danger."

"Don't worry about it," I say. "It's not your fault. Those super-Sheelds I told you about must have blocked our connection. Anyway, that's why we're here, to get rid of this problem once and for all."

You see, the Emperor made a big mistake. He told me he was genetically engineering Sheelds to control the Meta population. With superheroes out of the way, there wouldn't be anyone left to stop him from taking over Earth.

Unfortunately, he told the wrong person.

Because I'm here to destroy his super-Sheeld lab.

I take a look around to get my bearings. I figured if the White House had secret sub-levels, the Pentagon had them too. And according to my Geo-Locator device, we're actually standing in an 'unknown' level below ground that's not marked on any blueprints. This would be the perfect location for the Emperor's secret lab. And based on what I'm seeing, we've definitely worm-holed to the right place.

That's because everything around us screams laboratory, from the workstations covered with scientific equipment to the blackboards filled with crazy looking math equations. Thankfully, no one else is here at the moment, but the steaming coffee mug on a nearby desk tells me it won't stay that way for long.

"We've got to move," I say to Wind Walker.

I return the Geo-Locator to my utility belt and adjust my mask. It's good to be back in costume. Without it, I felt more like a super spy than a superhero. But now that I'm back in action, the Emperor is gonna pay big time.

I wish we could have brought the others, but it was too risky. Our mission requires stealth and the more people we had with us, the higher the chances of getting caught. That's why it's just me and Wind Walker—there's simply too much at stake.

However, it's not like the others are just sitting around. They're on an important mission of their own. Since Krule also commands an armada of mercenaries called the Motley Crew, we're going to need reinforcements. And with the Freedom Force missing, I tasked the Zodiac with finding help outside of Earth. Thankfully, they agreed to drop Next Gen back at their treehouse before they left.

Needless to say, my three new friends were pretty upset with me. Skunk Girl looked like she wanted to throttle me. But they all knew this mission was way over their heads, and the last thing I needed was for something bad to happen to them—like Dog-Gone.

I feel tears coming on, but I push them aside. I need to keep it together. Besides, he'd want me to stay focused right now. But for some reason, I can't stop thinking about Selfie.

When I tried saying goodbye, she caught me off guard and asked me if I was sending her home because Gemini showed up. I told her that wasn't it at all, but I'm not sure she believed me.

What's wrong with girls anyway?

"Epic Zero?" Wind Walker says. "Are you okay?"

"What?" I say, realizing I've been lost in my own thoughts. "Yeah, sorry."

There's a door on each end of the room, and I'm not sure which way to go. Wind Walker checks out one side while I take the other. When I get to my door, I hold the doorknob tight to prevent anyone from barging through and then place my ear against the surface.

I can't hear anything, but to my surprise, the door is cold. That's when I realize it's metal. But it's not just any metal, it's tungsten steel. I wave Wind Walker over.

"Was your door metal?" I ask.

"No," he says. "It's wood."

"Bingo," I say. "Something is behind this door."

The reason I know this is because TechnocRat always conducts his most dangerous experiments behind tungsten steel doors. So, I'm guessing there is something serious brewing behind this one. And it just might be what we're looking for.

"On the count of three," I whisper, ready to throw the door wide open and jump in.

"On the count of three, what?" Wind Walker whispers back. "There could be guards in there. We must be cautious."

Boy, I hope there are guards in there. I mean, I want nothing more than to avenge my pup. But he's right. If we're discovered too early, it will compromise everything.

"Fine," I whisper. "We'll go in cautiously. Ready? One… two…"

On three, I turn the door handle and pull, but it's so heavy I can't get it open. Fortunately, Wind Walker jumps in to help, and with considerable effort, we crack it wide enough for the two of us to slip through. Then, we lean against it to prevent it from slamming shut.

By the time the door clicks softly closed, I'm a sweaty mess. But before I can even turn around, Wind Walker grabs me and pulls me behind a stack of crates.

"You will be seen," he whispers.

"Sorry," I whisper back, feeling foolish.

I peek around the crates to find we're hiding in a stark, white room with hundreds of vials neatly organized on open shelves—and each vial contains a brown, leathery object floating in a purplish, bubbling liquid.

Super-Sheelds!

Some of them are smaller than my pinky, while others are bigger than a baseball mitt. But in the center of the room is the largest super-Sheeld I've ever seen.

It's thick, bloated, and bigger than an oven, with all of these wires sticking out of it. And next to the giant super-Sheeld is a metal table with arm and leg restraints.

There's no mistaking it.

We've found the genetic engineering lab.

But then I see something I didn't notice before. Sitting on the metal table is a strange-looking helmet. It's gold with mini circuits running all around the rim. It kind of looks like a futuristic motorcycle helmet.

What's that for?

"Now what?" Wind Walker asks.

"Now," I say, "we blow stuff up."

But just as I'm about to stand up, Wind Walker grabs me again and pulls me back.

"Wait," he whispers, "someone is coming."

Just then, a door on the opposite side of the room opens and three people walk in. I see a man and a woman who are wearing white lab coats, and another man who makes my blood boil. General Winch!

"Is everything prepared?" Winch asks.

"The calculations are set," the female scientist says. "We do not anticipate any more errors."

"Is that so?" Winch says, sounding skeptical. "Because your last 'error' resulted in the death of one of the Meta specimens."

My heart skips a beat. Did he say, 'death?'

What if it was Mom or Dad? Or Grace?

I desperately want to charge out there and force Winch to tell me who it was, but I know I can't. If we reveal ourselves too soon, Winch will call an army of Meta-Busters so fast it'll make our heads spin.

"The Emperor will not be pleased to hear the news," Winch continues. "As a result of your idiocy, we have lost another thirty milligrams of Meta energy that could have been used to harvest more advanced Sheelds. I would be surprised if the Emperor lets you live."

"Please, General," the male scientist pleads. "We beg of you, do not inform the Emperor of our mistake. The biochemistry of every Meta is different. It is simply impossible to predict how each one will react to the leeching process. You must protect us. We will do anything you ask."

Leeching process?

Hang on. The Emperor mentioned something about a leeching process back in the Oval Office.

I mean, I know what leeches do here on Earth. They're earthworm-like creatures that can attach to your skin and suck your blood. So, is that what that monster super-Sheeld is being used for? Except instead of blood, it's sucking the Meta energy out of superheroes.

"Anything?" Winch says, his left eyebrow rising. "Very well, but be warned, if I spare you from the Emperor, you must do as I command, no matter what I ask of you. Even if it is against the Emperor's wishes. Do you agree?"

"Against the Emperor's wishes?" the female scientist says. "But that is forbidden."

For a second, Winch looks so angry I think he's going to strike her, but instead, he furrows his brow, and the next thing I know, he transforms from a skinny, regular-sized human into a gigantic armored warrior with bulging muscles, yellow skin, and pointy ears.

OMG!

Winch is… a Skelton?

I'm flabbergasted.

But then again, I guess I shouldn't be, because it makes total sense. Winch always wanted to get rid of Meta heroes, and now I know why!

"Very well," Winch says, turning to the exit. "I was only trying to spare your lives. But if that is your choice than I must go speak with the Emperor at once. As I am the High Commander of the Blood Bringer army, do not be surprised when I return at the Emperor's command to kill you with my own hands. I will leave you now to enjoy your final moments."

The two scientists look at one another, and then—

"Wait!" the male scientist calls out. "Do not go. We agree. We will do as you say."

"You have made a wise decision," Winch says, turning around. "Now bring in our next specimen. I will supervise your work on this one myself. After all, she is critical for the success of my plan."

As the scientists exit the room, I look over at Wind Walker who shrugs his shoulders. Who could Winch be talking about?

But when I turn back my stomach sinks.

Because the 'specimen' the scientists are carrying into the room is Mom!

TWELVE

I CAN'T SEEM TO AVOID DANGER

I can't believe it!

Mom is unconscious, and Winch and the male scientist are hooking her into the table restraints while the female scientist is putting that strange, futuristic-looking helmet on her head!

It takes everything I've got not to jump in to save her, but my instincts are telling me to wait. I don't know why, but I feel like I should trust my gut. So, before Wind Walker springs into action, I put my hand on his shoulder and my finger to my lips.

"She is secure," Winch says, locking the final ankle restraint in place. "And remember the Emperor's orders, do not activate the leeching process for Psychics. They are too valuable to lose if something goes wrong."

"Yes, we remember," the male scientist says, holding up a pair of wires attached to the giant super-Sheeld. "We will set these transfer cables aside."

Okay, that pretty much confirms it. That massive super-Sheeld is some kind of leech, and they're using it to steal Meta powers.

"The B-Mod unit is fully charged," the female scientist says, checking some dials on a computer terminal.

B-Mod unit? What's that?

Then, it hits me! 'B-Mod' could only be short for one thing—behavior modification! And that helmet on Mom's head must be a behavior modification device!

"We can begin the brain override sequence," the female scientist says. "But I must warn you, it is dangerous to employ behavior modification on a Psychic like this without first implementing the leeching process to erase her powers. Anything could happen."

"No leeching!" Winch commands. "Now get on with it. Just ensure you do not accidentally kill this one."

Um, did he just say, 'kill?'

"The Meta-human's biochemistry will determine if she survives the stress or not," the woman says, walking back over to fix Mom's helmet. Then, she reaches for a green button.

Okay, I've heard enough.

"Hands off!" I yell, leaping out from behind the crates. And with one fluid motion, I reach into my utility belt and throw my brand-new Epic-a-rang—which is my E-shaped version of Shadow Hawk's Hawk-a-rang—right at the woman's hand. There, that should put an end to this dastardly scheme.

But the Epic-a-rang whizzes over the woman's head and CLANGS harmlessly against the wall.

"What kind of a fool are you?" the woman asks.

Well, that was embarrassing.

But at least she didn't push the button on Mom's helmet.

"So, we meet again," Winch says, as a strange smile creeps across his face. "I thought you might come here, but I never expected you to succeed."

"Well, I guess it's a day full of surprises," I say.

Speaking of surprises, I quickly glance down at Wind Walker, but he's gone! I swallow hard. I hope he didn't have to use the bathroom.

"Indeed, child," Winch says, stepping towards me. "This day will be filled with more surprises than you ever imagined."

Um, I don't know what he means by that, but I do know one thing, he's way bigger than any Skelton I've faced before. And that's saying something because I've fought more of these buggers than I care to remember.

Maybe I should start wearing alien repellent spray.

But I've got an even bigger problem. I don't have a plan. And based on experience, things don't go well when I don't have a plan.

I'll need to bluff until I can figure something out.

"Let that hero go," I demand, pointing to Mom. "And no one will get hurt."

Laughter fills the room.

"Hey!" I say. "I'm serious."

"The only creature who will be hurt," Winch says, cracking his knuckles, "is you. I have been waiting for this moment ever since our meeting at the television studio. If I had only known then what I know now, I would have eliminated you on the spot. But then again, it appears you are not so easy to kill, because you narrowly escaped from your satellite headquarters before my Meta-Busters could finish the job."

Um, before *his* Meta-Busters could finish the job?

Suddenly, I connect the dots.

When I was on the Waystation, a group of Meta-Busters went rogue and blasted one of their own trying to kill me. And based on what he's saying, Winch must have put them up to that, despite the Emperor's wishes!

But why?

"Um, sorry," I say. "But what did I ever do to you?"

"It is not what you did," Winch says, "but rather, what you could do. You see, the Emperor has put great faith in your ability to defeat Krule the Conqueror. He believes that once Krule is finally out of the way, he will be free to rule the universe with an iron fist. But he has greatly miscalculated."

Suddenly, behind Winch, a black circle appears over

the scientists' heads. And then two blue arms reach down and pull the scientists up into the void!

It's Wind Walker!

"The Emperor does not realize the tides have turned," Winch continues, oblivious to what's happening behind him. "As soon as he gave the order to flee from our Homeworld rather than fight our greatest enemy, Krule the Conqueror, he lost the support of his loyal subjects. Just as I planned."

A second later, the void disappears.

"The Emperor has disgraced the Skelton Empire," Winch says. "Unlike our great leaders of the past who valued strength over cowardice and domination over subservience, the Emperor values nothing but himself. His removal from power is long overdue. But I could never risk acting on our Homeworld. After all, I am not of royal blood, and he was always surrounded by too many minions who could have thwarted my plan. But unfortunately for them, I was in charge of our escape pods, and I ensured that I was the only surviving member of the Emperor's inner circle to make it to Earth alive."

Well, note to self. This guy is way more psycho than I gave him credit for. And that's saying something!

"It is time for a leader who will restore glory to the Skelton Empire," Winch continues, "and I am the one who will do so. Thus, when an unthinkable alliance presented itself, only I was bold enough to take full advantage where others in my position would have run."

Unthinkable alliance? Um, what unthinkable alliance?

"Nothing will stand in my way," he says, raising his right arm, "Including you!"

Suddenly, Winch swings down and I dive out of the way as his giant fist sends floor tiles flying! Okay, he's really strong! And then I remember Winch saying he's the High Commander of the Blood Bringer army.

I'm gonna need help!

Just then, a void opens up next to Winch and Wind Walker leaps out, his fist reared back for the knock-out blow.

Yes!

But just as quickly, Winch leans out of the way and Wind Walker goes sailing past.

No!

Then, with incredible speed, Winch delivers a devastating roundhouse kick, sending Wind Walker headfirst into the wall. Wind Walker hits with a sickening thud and then crumples to the ground unconscious.

"Now it's your turn," Winch says.

I'm about to hit him with a major dose of negation power when Winch grabs a vial from one of the shelves and chucks it at me!

I dive out of the way as the vial zips over my head and SHATTERS into the wall behind me. I cover my head as glass flies everywhere and a super-Sheeld flops to the ground.

Holy cow! He's throwing super-Sheelds at me!

Now I'm not much of a dodgeball player, but if those super-Sheelds touch me, I'll lose my powers! But before I can get up, Winch grabs another vial and winds up for another pitch. I throw myself behind a computer terminal as the vial SMASHES into the wall behind me.

My heart is pounding out of my chest. I've got to stay calm. If I don't handle this wacko now, I might not get a second chance to save Mom.

Then, I realize it's quiet.

Why is it so darn quiet?

RRROOOAARRR!

Um, what's that?

Just then, a massive hairy, white fist reaches around the computer terminal! I make like a pancake, pressing flat against the wall as four giant fingers try pulling me into a death grip! What is that thing? Then, I realize this must be one of the forms Winch can morph into!

I've got to get out of here!

But the next thing I know, six paws wrap around the terminal and toss it aside like it was a tissue box. The terminal SMASHES into another bank of computers and CRASHES to the ground, barely missing Wind Walker's still unconscious body.

Now nothing is standing between me and Winch! Except Winch looks like a cross between the Abominable Snowman and a spider.

Did I ever mention that I hate spiders?

My mind goes through some quick mental

gymnastics. Either I can stick around to fight monster-Winch, or I can go into flight mode and get the heck out of here!

Winch opens his mouth and ROARS!

Well, that settles it. It's flight time! My eyes dart around the room, looking for an escape route. Then, they land on Wind Walker.

Desperate times call for desperate measures! So, I focus my duplication powers on Wind Walker's prone body and copy his powers. Then, just as Winch reaches for me with his six overgrown mitts, I create a void, jump inside, and I'm gone.

Suddenly, I'm standing high above him in a wormhole, looking down as he spins around in circles trying to find me. Boy, it's strange how everything around me looks blurry like I'm speeding past in a subway car. Yet, I'm standing completely still. Winch has no idea where I went, and it would be super easy to just take off, except there's no way I'm leaving here by myself.

As I step gingerly through Wind Walker's wormhole, I realize everything is different. I mean, when Wind Walker pulls me through one of these things it's always a roller-coaster experience. But now that I'm in control, everything seems so much calmer. That's when I look down and see Mom's blurry body.

She's still lying on the table, down for the count. I check on Winch who is still raging on the other side of the room. Now's my chance. I bend down and reach through the wormhole, grabbing Mom beneath her arms. Then, I deadlift her up to safety. Ugh! My back feels like it's broken but I got her. I just hope she's okay.

"Mom," I say, gently patting her cheek. "Can you hear me?"

She moans.

Then, I realize she's still wearing that funky helmet. I try pulling it off but it's stuck. Okay, this will have to wait. I've still got one more person to rescue.

I crawl to the other side of the wormhole and look down. Winch is searching the room more carefully now, even pulling panels off of computers to look inside. After struggling to get Mom, there's no way I'm gonna be able to lift Wind Walker.

But then I realize I don't have to. After all, I've seen him project his voids across great distances to swallow up his victims. So, I concentrate hard, creating a void right over Wind Walker's entire body.

RROOARR!

It's Winch! He's looking up! I need to act fast!

I drop the void over Wind Walker's body like a drape and he disappears. Then, I grab Mom's hand to do the same when Winch jumps up and rips open a swath of ceiling right next to us!

OMG! He knows we're up here!

So, I wrap my arms around Mom and make us disappear!

THIRTEEN

I MAKE THE RULES

We POP out in the woods and I drop to my knees in a jumbled mix of exhaustion and disbelief.

I mean, everything that just happened was nuts!

Winch is a Skelton, there's an entire lab of super-Sheelds sucking away Meta powers, and a Meta died during the leeching process! I'm so overwhelmed I don't even know what to do.

"E-Elliott?" comes a feeble voice.

"Mom!" I blurt out, crawling to her side. She's lying on the ground with that futuristic helmet on her head. "Are you okay? Please tell me you're okay."

"I-I'm fine," she says, sitting up. She looks groggy, but when she finally regains her wits, she wraps me up in a big hug. "Oh, Elliott, I'm so happy to see you."

As I fall into her embrace, tears stream down my

cheeks and I start bawling like a baby.

"Hey," she says, holding my chin. "It'll be okay. Now tell me what's going on."

"I-I...," I stammer, but I'm so choked up I can't even speak. But with Mom, I don't have to, because she looks me in the eyes, and in an instant, she's mind-read the whole thing.

"Oh, Elliott, I'm so sorry," she says, hugging me again. "Dog-Gone was a brave hero and a good friend."

"Yeah," I say, wiping away my tears. "The best. Even though he was really annoying."

"Yes, but he was the best kind of annoying," she says.

We chuckle, and it feels good to laugh again, but the moment is cut short when I hear—

"Epic Zero," Wind Walker says, sitting up with his head in his hands. "What happened?"

"Are you okay?" I ask. "You got clobbered by Winch. But I used your wormhole powers to get us all to safety."

"You did?" he says surprised. "Well done, my friend." Then, he looks up and says, "but I think our troubles are just beginning."

Huh? What's he talking about? But when I look up, I see hundreds of dots in the sky. What are those things? They seem too high to be birds, but then my stomach drops as I realize those aren't birds at all.

They're spaceships!

Krule and his Motley Crew have arrived!

I hear SHOUTING to my left and when I look over,

I can see the Pentagon through the trees. It's total chaos over there as soldiers are running every which way while Meta-Busters are assembling on the roof. It looks like they're trying to mount a defense.

But as I look back up, I realize something is not right. I remember Winch telling the Emperor it would take weeks for Krule to get here. How could he be so wrong?

And then I remember Winch talking about his 'unthinkable alliance,' and a lightbulb goes off.

Winch was lying to the Emperor!

Winch has partnered with Krule the Conqueror!

That's his 'unthinkable alliance!'

"What is this thing?" Mom says, touching the helmet. She tries yanking it off of her head, but it doesn't budge. Then, she twists it and it pops right off.

"That's a Skelton behavior modification device," I say. "The Skelton have been using it to brainwash heroes."

"Not this hero," Mom says, tossing it over her shoulder. "Thanks to you. And if what I learned from reading your mind is true, these spaceships aren't here for a friendly visit. We're going to need help to send them back where they came from. Fortunately, I know where the rest of the Freedom Force is located, but I'll have to sneak back inside the Pentagon. Do you think you'll be safe here until I get back?"

"There is no need to sneak," Wind Walker says. "I can take you there directly."

"Wait," I say. "What about me? I want to come."

"No, Elliott," Mom says, standing up. "We can't... I mean, I can't risk it. Look, getting me out alive was lucky enough, but I'm not sure what's happened to Dad or Grace. And if something did happen... Well, I'm not ready to lose you too. Please, just wait here for me."

The concern in her eyes squashes my soul.

I mean, I get it. I just lost Dog-Gone and I'm absolutely gutted. And I certainly don't want anything to happen to Dad or Grace either, but I just can't sit here twiddling my thumbs while either Krule or the Emperor take over our planet. After all, sitting on the sidelines is what got me into this mess in the first place.

"Ten minutes," I say firmly, crossing my arms.

"Elliott—"

"No, Mom," I say. "You've got ten minutes. If I don't see or hear from you guys in ten minutes, then I've gotta do what I've gotta do. Look, I've more than proven I can take care of myself. I know it's easy to forget sometimes, but I destroyed the Orb of Oblivion, got rid of Ravager, and just saved the two of you. So, I know I'm still a kid and all, but I'm a hero, just like you."

"You're right," Mom says, giving me another hug. "But you're not just any hero, you're a great hero. However, I'm still your mom, so if I'm not back in ten minutes don't do anything stupid."

Then, she takes Wind Walker's hand, and they disappear into a wormhole.

Okay, the countdown starts now.

But as I look back up, the spaceships have gotten way closer! In fact, I can see the first few pretty clearly now and none of them look the same. One is long and thin and shaped like a 'Y,' while another is round and stout and shaped like an 'O.' I guess that's why Krule calls them 'the Motley Crew,' because they're just a ragtag gang of degenerates from across the galaxy.

But that's not all that's happening, because when I look over at the Pentagon, they seem much more organized. Soldiers are standing in formation next to heavy artillery, and the Meta-Busters are rocketing into the sky in well-organized battalions. But then I see something else. There, standing at the edge of the roof, are two figures I know all too well—General Winch and the Emperor!

I reach into my utility belt and pull out my binoculars. Winch is standing behind the Emperor, pointing to the sky, while the Emperor is looking up with his hands clasped behind his back. They look like partners in crime, but the Emperor has no clue Winch has betrayed him.

Okay, I figure five minutes have gone by and there is no sign of Mom or Wind Walker.

I carefully pick my way through the underbrush and hide behind a thick tree to get a better vantage point. But when I peer around the trunk, my foot CLANGS against something solid. Hmm, rocks don't make noises like that.

But when I reach down to investigate, I pull up

Mom's helmet. That's funny, I almost forgot about it. I turn it in my hands, studying it closely. I've got no clue what all of these Skelton symbols mean, but I do recognize the green button that scientist was going to push to turn it on.

For a second I nearly chuck it, but then I decide to hold onto it. Who knows? It may come in handy.

Okay, the ten minutes have to be up by now.

Where's Mom? I hope she's okay. But if she's in trouble I never asked her where she was going in the first place, which means it'll be impossible for me to find her.

I smack my palm against my forehead.

How many other 'great heroes' are idiots like me?

Suddenly, there's a massive explosion overhead and when I look up, parts of a Meta-Buster are raining down from the sky. Uh-oh, it's started! And even though the ten minutes have passed I don't know what to do next.

I look through my binoculars again and do a double take because Winch is still standing behind the Emperor, but now he's pulling a knife out from beneath his armored vest!

He's literally going to backstab the Emperor!

For a second, I hesitate. I mean, would it be so bad if the Emperor was a goner? But then my conscience takes over. I can't just sit here watching a murder unfold right before my eyes. But how can I stop Winch from here?

And then I remember something.

I just used Wind Walker's powers, and if I still have

some juice left, I should be able to get over there in time.

So, I concentrate hard and summon a void.

And then I step inside.

FOURTEEN

I JUST WANNA FLY

I reach the roof of the Pentagon in the nick of time!

I'm about a dozen feet behind Winch, who is still drawing his knife behind the Emperor's back! And even though the firefight above sounds like the Fourth of July, I don't want to give myself away, so I step gingerly out of the void.

For a split second, I contemplate jumping Winch and wresting the knife away, but after taking one look at his broad shoulders I decide against it. Instead, I'm about to call out to the Emperor when I hear—

"My Meta-Busters are failing," the Emperor says.

"What a pity," Winch says, his long knife now fully exposed. "I had designed them to fight."

"And yet, it appears they are giving up," the Emperor says. "Why are they giving up, General?"

Giving up? But as I steal a glance at the sky, I see he's right! The Meta-Busters are actually flying away from the fight, giving Krule's army a clear path to Earth.

"Maybe they no longer want to fight for you?" Winch says, raising the knife over his head.

Oh no! This is really about to happen!

"Emperor!" I yell. "Look out!"

But instead of striking down the Emperor, Winch spins around to face me, the knife still over his head!

"You!" he says, looking at me wild-eyed.

"There you are, child," the Emperor says, turning to face us both. Strangely, he looks completely calm. In fact, if I didn't know better, I'd think he was... grinning? "Thank you for the warning, but it was not necessary. I had the situation well under control."

"You spineless fool!" Winch says, spit flying from his mouth as he turns back to the Emperor. "You have control of nothing! You are the most pathetic leader in the history of the Skelton Empire! Today I will save our people from your cowardly reign! Today there will be a change in power, and my blade will deliver it!"

"Ah, yes, your blade," the Emperor says, eyeing Winch's knife. "It *is* quite impressive. In fact, is it not the Knife of Terrors you wield—the very same knife I bestowed upon you when I appointed you as Head Commander of the Blood Bringer Army?"

"Y-Yes?" Winch says, his eyes growing wide as he looks upon his knife.

"I thought so," the Emperor says, breaking into a sinister smile.

FAZZZZZAAAMMM!

Suddenly, a massive surge of electricity bursts from the hilt of Winch's knife. I shield my eyes from the blinding light and turn away as my body is blanketed by an intense wave of heat. And when it finally subsides, I look back to find a charred body lying where Winch used to be standing.

"You-You killed him," I say.

"I did, didn't I?" the Emperor says, holding some kind of a device in his hand. "But he knew it was coming. After all, he did murder my entire council of advisors. Of course, I respected his ruthlessness for that little maneuver, but I never trusted him. That is why I secretly outfitted the Knife of Terrors with nearly ten thousand volts of electricity before I gave it to him. Fortunately, I keep the activator handy in my belt. Poor Winch. He had potential, but he never quite learned that cunning always beats strength in the end."

"But he wasn't acting alone," I say. "He was working with—"

"—me," comes a deep voice from behind that sends shivers down my spine.

I swallow hard. I don't want to turn around, but I have to. And when I do, it feels like someone sucked all of the air out of my lungs, because standing in front of me is the biggest, baddest villain in the entire multiverse.

Krule the Conqueror.

"I must thank you for disposing of Winch," Krule says to the Emperor. "He was useful but far too needy. Now I can focus on my primary objective, which is ridding the universe of you."

"I am sure you would like that," the Emperor says. "But I am afraid I have other ideas."

The two are facing off like they're in an alien version of an old Western movie—and I'm stuck in the middle!

"You are filled with clever ideas, aren't you?" Krule says. "Like how you tricked me into entering the 13th Dimension."

"You might consider it trickery," the Emperor says. "I would call it masterful plotting."

"You violated our agreement," Krule says. "You were to rule your side of the universe and I was to rule mine. Yet, that was not enough for you, was it? You had to have it all to yourself."

"I am far from naive," the Emperor says. "Did you really think I believed that someone named Krule the Conqueror would settle for half of anything? You see, we are not so unalike. I knew your thirst for power would be your undoing. All I did was plant the seed by bribing one of your underlings to pretend he discovered the coordinates to a new universe. I believe Xenox was his name. He was a shifty character, but once he delivered the coordinates, I knew you could not resist your animal instincts to conquer an entirely new universe.

Unfortunately, those coordinates just happened to belong to the 13th Dimension."

"You hoped to trap me in that barren wasteland forever," Krule says. "But my unrivaled power transcended even that forsaken place. I only wish I could have seen the look on your face when you heard of my escape—when you realized I would be coming to destroy you."

"Well, I admit I was surprised you even wanted to leave," the Emperor says. "I figured the 13th Dimension was a perfect match for your lifeless personality."

"Enough!" Krule says, his third eye glowing green. "No more games. You may have escaped when I conquered your Homeworld, but now there is nowhere left to run."

"Perhaps not," the Emperor says, buffing his nails. "But there is no need to run. Not with my champion here to protect me."

"Champion?" Krule says. "What champion?"

"The child," the Emperor says. "He is my champion."

Um, what?

"Ha!" Krule chuckles. "You must be joking."

"No," the Emperor says. "I am certainly not joking. The child's powers dwarf even yours. In fact, I believe he would beat you handily in a fight to the death."

"Whoa!" I say, stepping forward. "I never agreed to that."

"Forgive my 'champion,'" the Emperor says to Krule.

"He must have forgotten that if you destroy me, you will conquer his planet and turn all of its inhabitants into mindless slaves. Isn't that correct, 'Champion?'"

I want to say, 'no way,' but I know he's right. At the moment, the Emperor is actually the lesser of two evils. If I'm gonna save everyone on Earth, I have no choice but to stand and fight Krule first—maybe even to the death.

"Very well," Krule says, eyeing me up and down in triplicate, "I accept your challenge. After all, I always relish a good appetizer before feasting upon the main course. I will destroy the child, and then I will destroy you."

"Excellent," the Emperor says, backing away. "Good luck, 'Champion.' And do not forget what I taught you."

What he taught me? But suddenly Krule turns his massive frame my way and it's hard to remember anything!

"I know you," Krule says. "You were tangling with the Time Trotter, trying to stop me from obtaining the Cosmic Key."

"Yep, that was me alright," I say, backing up. "I was just, you know, doing what heroes are supposed to do."

"That is amusing," Krule says, "because where I come from, what heroes are supposed to do is die!"

Suddenly, Krule's third eye glows green and I hit the panic button. I mean, this is Krule the freaking Conqueror—the most powerful Psychic ever! If he can take over hundreds of people at once, I'm about to get hammered! I need to protect myself!

I send my duplication powers at Krule and pull them back quickly, but the massive power surge throws my system off balance! Holy smokes! I only grabbed an ounce of his power, so if this is a taste of what's to come, I'm in serious trouble!

Just then, I feel incredible pressure in my head!

Submit.

It's Krule! He's burrowing inside my brain!

I hear a CLANKING noise and when I look down, I see the behavior modification helmet hit the edge of the roof and roll off. Honestly, I forgot I was even holding that thing!

Submit, child.

No! Never!

I push him out, but it's only for a second and the pressure starts building again. He's way too powerful. I can't sustain this. I need to try something else.

That's when I spot the Emperor slinking into the corner. That coward! He's trying to escape!

Not on my watch!

I concentrate hard, pushing Krule out of my head with all I've got. Then, I focus all of my power on the Emperor, bathing him with duplication energy. I need to absorb as much of the Emperor's shape-shifting powers as I can! If I can just morph into one of those crazy creatures like Winch, then maybe I've got half a chance against Krule!

But when I pull the Emperor's Meta energy back, I barely feel anything. Huh? That's weird. And when I cycle through the Emperor's rolodex of bizarre and scary creatures, there's almost nothing!

In fact, all I'm getting are human shapes or… flies?

What's going on? Then, it hits me.

K'ami once told me there are two types of Skelton: regular Skelton, who can morph into a few forms, or Blood Bringers, who can change into anything imaginable. And I did run into that souped-up Blood Bringer called a Blood Master a few times.

But to my surprise, the Emperor isn't a Blood Bringer or a Blood Master! Which can only mean one thing—he's just an ordinary, run-of-the-mill Skelton!

OMG! I wonder if the other Skelton know that, or if the Emperor has been fooling them all of this time?

Now I know why he needed me to defeat Krule for him! The high and mighty Emperor is nothing but a fraud!

But I can't worry about that. Right now, I need to focus on survival! If I can get some distance to regroup, I can come up with a plan. So, I take what I've got and morph into a fly. Then, I buzz off.

Beating my wings is a bit awkward at first, but I quickly get the hang of it. But as soon as I clear the roofline and head towards the woods, I hear—

Nice try, but you cannot escape my power.

Suddenly, my head feels like it's on fire!

Krule is pushing his way inside again! It's... hard to concentrate... on flying. I try forcing him out, but he's too strong.

And then I feel myself turning against my will.

What's happening?

Then, it dawns on me. In fly form, my brain has shrunken to the size of a poppy seed. It's... harder to keep him... out! And Krule is... manipulating the part of my brain that controls my... motor skills!

I've got to... stay strong. Push him... out!

Come. Come back to me.

Just then, my whole body jerks left and my wings start beating even faster. No! Stop it! Let... me go!

I try flying away, but he's bringing me right back up to the roof! And once he sees me, he'll squash me!

I-I need to go...

... down?

Then, a lightbulb goes off.

The only reason I'm flying back towards Krule is because I have wings.

This might not be the best idea, but what other choice do I have? So, I concentrate hard and let the Emperor's shapeshifting powers go. Suddenly, my wings retract and my body morphs back into a full-sized kid.

Then, I drop like a rock.

I need to stop my fall!

I reach into my utility belt for my grappling gun when I realize I left it on the Waystation.

That's not good.
I'm falling to my doom!
Four stories.
I'm picking up speed!
Three stories.
I flap my arms to slow my fall.
Two stories.
Everything goes blurry.
And all I see is black.

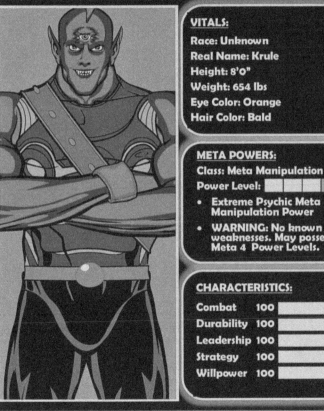

Meta Profile

Name: Krule the Conqueror
Role: Villain   Status: Active

VITALS:
Race: Unknown
Real Name: Krule
Height: 8'0"
Weight: 654 lbs
Eye Color: Orange
Hair Color: Bald

META POWERS:
Class: Meta Manipulation
Power Level:
- Extreme Psychic Meta Manipulation Power
- WARNING: No known weaknesses. May possess Meta 4 Power Levels.

CHARACTERISTICS:
Combat	100
Durability	100
Leadership	100
Strategy	100
Willpower	100

FIFTEEN

I FACE DOUBLE TROUBLE

"Elliott."

I hear a faint noise in the distance.

"Elliott."

Repeating itself. Getting louder. Strangely familiar.

Wait a second. Why does this all seem so familiar?

Suddenly, the hairs on the back of my neck stand on end and my eyes jolt open. It's dark and misty, but I can make out the shape of someone walking towards me in the distance.

It's… a girl?

My instincts are telling me to run, but for some reason, I can't move a muscle. I can blink and breathe just fine, but my limbs are frozen. But as the girl gets closer, the only thing I can make out are her eyes.

Her neon, green… eyes?

Then, she steps out of the darkness, and my jaw drops in disbelief. OMG! It… it can't be!

"K'ami?" I say.

But that's impossible! Except, the girl standing in front of me looks exactly like her. My eyes dart from her pretty face to her pointy ears, to the dark ringlets falling over her shoulders. She's even wearing the same outfit I saw her in last—all white with gold trim!

I must be dreaming, but when I shut my eyes and open them again, she's still standing there.

"K'ami?" I repeat. "Is that really you?"

"Yes, Elliott Harkness," she says, her voice echoing all around us.

"B-But…," I stammer. "You're dead!"

"That is true," she says.

"So," I say, looking around the darkness, "does that mean I'm dead too?"

"No, Elliott Harkness," she says. "Not yet. But if you keep this up, you will be soon."

"Um, okay," I say. "Then, where am I?"

"You are in a place called the 'In Between,'" K'ami says. "A place that exists neither in life nor in death. But we don't have much time. I'm only able to hold you here momentarily."

"Hold me here?" I say. "What are you talking about? I mean, if you're dead, how are you even doing this?"

"You can thank the Orb of Oblivion," she says.

The words send a chill down my spine. I mean, the

Orb of Oblivion is what got her killed in the first place.

"I see your confusion, so let me explain," she continues. "As I lay dying in your arms, I was holding the Orb of Oblivion. As you know, the Orb of Oblivion has the power to fulfill the desires of its host. And although I knew it was too late to save me, I asked the Orb for one final request. I asked it for the power to save you."

"What?" I blurt out. "Are you serious?"

"Yes," she says. "The Orb agreed, but I'm sure it did so only to serve its own selfish needs in case something dreadful happened to you. But it granted me the power nonetheless—the power to save you one time and one time only."

"But that's not possible," I say. "Is it?"

"I questioned it as well," she says. "Especially once I moved beyond the living, but it appears that it has worked because here I am in your greatest time of need."

"K'ami," I say, tears suddenly squirting from my eyes. "I'm so sorry for everything that happened. I-I should have seen it coming. I should have taken the Orb from you. I shouldn't have let you…"

"It is okay, Elliott Harkness," K'ami says, smiling gently. "I am at peace, and I am proud of you. I believed in you in a time when you didn't believe in yourself, and now look at all of the good you have done."

"B-But K'ami," I blubber. "I… I can't do this. Krule is too strong. The guy is a psychopath. And he's—"

"—powerful," K'ami says, finishing my sentence.

"Just like you. Never forget the power you possess. Inside of here," she says, pointing to my head. "But most importantly," she says, now pointing to my heart, "inside of here."

"But K'ami," I plead. "I don't know how..."

"Yes," she says, smiling. "You do. You know exactly how to defeat him. Now it is time for you to return."

Then, she reaches out and touches my temple, but strangely I don't feel any pressure against my head.

Instead, a light breeze tickles my hair.

"Go back, Elliott Harkness," she says. "Go back and use all that you have learned. And remember, never show weakness."

Suddenly, my eyelids feel super heavy.

They start closing, but I don't want to lose her again!

Yet, no matter how hard I fight to keep them open, I can't. I open my mouth to beg her not to leave me again, but no words come out.

And then everything goes...

***

...dark.

I feel groggy like I've been napping for hours. I press my hands down and realize I'm lying on a hard surface that feels like concrete. Okay, I'm probably not splattered all over the pavement. So that means my dream about K'ami must have been real.

Holy smokes, she actually saved my life!

I open my eyes, hoping to gaze upon a peaceful, blue sky, but instead, I find a raging battle being waged overhead. Krule's Motley Crew are scattered all over the sky, but they're no longer fighting Meta-Busters. Instead, they're weaving through a cloud of orange specks that sort of look like … fireflies?

But then it hits me.

Those aren't fireflies.

They're Infinity Wands!

The Intergalactic Paladins are here!

So, that means—

Just then, a silver, submarine-shaped vehicle swerves behind one of Krule's ships and blasts it from behind, sending it towards Earth in a smoking death spiral.

It's the Ghost Ship!

Yes! The Zodiac did it! They actually recruited the Intergalactic Paladins to help! Suddenly, there's a blinding barrage of orange light as the Paladins go on the offensive with their Infinity Wands, knocking ship after ship out of the sky.

I can't believe it. The good guys are finally winning!

And I feel something I haven't felt in a while—hope.

But then my body is shrouded in a dark shadow.

"Stand and fight, 'Champion,'" Krule says in a mocking tone. "Show me this vast power your master has bragged about. Unless, of course, you are afraid."

Oh, jeez. Back to reality!

I scramble to my feet and face Krule, my neck craning back to take him all in. He's an absolute giant, towering over me with his arms crossed and a smirk lining his smug face. Honestly, I don't think I've ever met a scarier looking dude, but for some reason, this time I'm not feeling so scared.

In fact, I'm feeling downright angry.

K'ami's last words echo in my head—*use all that you have learned*—and suddenly, I know exactly what to do.

Principle number one: Never show weakness.

"I'm not afraid of you," I say, my hands on my hips.

"That is a mistake," Krule says, his third eye flickering green. "Most likely, your last."

Principle number two: Always go on the offensive.

I concentrate hard, and then project my powers up into the sky, pushing them further than I've ever pushed them before, reaching out for every single Intergalactic Paladin in flight. And then I duplicate the power of a hundred Infinity Wands at once!

The energy surge is massive!

My body feels super-charged, like pure electricity is coursing through my veins—and when I look down, orange sparks are dancing around my fingers!

I-I've never felt such immense power before. It feels like I'm floating on air, like I'm having an out-of-body experience. It feels like I might be at... Meta 4?

But it's way more power than I could ever hope to contain. Fortunately, I don't plan on keeping it.

I point my arms at Krule, and then I let him have it.

SZZAAAACCCKKKK!

The massive discharge knocks me clear off my feet, but not before I see the blast strike Krule full in the chest, blowing him straight through the concrete walls of the Pentagon. Debris flies everywhere as the entire building buckles and then collapses on top of him, sending a giant plume of dust into the air.

By now I'm lying flat on my back with orange smoke billowing off my hands. Wow, I wasn't expecting that, but I'll take it. I just hope he's down for the count.

Please let him be down for the count.

But as I get to my feet, massive chunks of concrete come flying back out of the hole, followed by a wave of office equipment. I dodge a conference table and duck beneath a stapler that zips over my head. Darn it, he's clearly not down for the count, and I guess he doesn't need to staple anything.

Okay, I'm in serious trouble. I mean, if a blast from a hundred Infinity Wands couldn't knock him out then what will? I need another solution and fast.

But as the dust settles, my heart skips a beat, because standing inside the ruins of the building is an eight-foot silhouette. Krule is coming back for more!

If I'm gonna win, I've got to think outside the box. I need to surprise him. Wait a second. Surprise!

That's principle number three!

Suddenly, I get a wild idea.

It may not work, but it's all I got. So, I bathe Krule in my duplication powers, grab some telekinesis, and then get down to business. I concentrate hard, sending Krule's power deep below the Pentagon.

"I have had enough," Krule says, his voice booming. "Your life ends now."

Well, that certainly sounds bad, but I can't risk diverting my focus. I keep pushing Krule's telekinesis downward, but there's just a ton of earth in the way. But I can't give up. Even though sweat is pouring down my face, stinging my eyes, I need to keep trying.

Then, out of the corner of my eye, I see Krule!

He's striding towards me, his third eye glowing.

Submit.

Aahh! There's a sharp pain inside my brain! He's getting inside my head! I need to... hold him off! But I... can't give him my full attention. I can't stop... doing what I'm doing.

You are strong, but I am so much stronger.

I glance over again and realize he's almost on top of me! He's raising his arms! He's not waiting for his mind control! He's gonna pound me with his fists!

This is it! Focus!

I bend down and give it everything I've got!

RRRIIIPPPPP!

Suddenly, the ground between us bursts wide open and a funnel of dirt spews out like lava from a volcano.

Krule's three eyes go wide and he steps back startled.

But I keep pulling because what I'm going for isn't dirt and rubble—it's super-Sheelds! Just then, the brown, leathery organisms pop out of the hole one by one, hovering in the air as I collect them between us—and then I send them at Krule like an army of killer bees!

Krule staggers back as the giant one slams into him first, latching onto his chest. And then the others pile on, covering every inch of Krule's massive body as they knock him to the ground, draining his power.

I did it! But I'm so exhausted I drop to my knees.

"Well done, Champion," comes a voice.

I turn to find the Emperor standing behind me, smiling like he's just won gold in the Evil-Olympics. Then, he reaches into his belt and pulls out a thin golden rod. What's that for? But with the mere push of a button, it extends on both sides into a long, sharp spear!

"Now it is time to execute principle number four," he says, offering the spear to me. "Show no mercy. Kill Krule before he recovers and kills you."

What? Kill Krule?

"Take the spear, my champion," the Emperor demands. "Finish the job before it is too late."

I stand up, my legs still wobbly. My brain hears what the Emperor is saying, but something doesn't feel right.

"Take it," the Emperor insists. "End his life."

I don't want to do it, but I know he's right. I mean, this might be my only chance to stop Krule for good.

I grab the spear.

"Excellent," the Emperor says. "Now, for the survival of your planet, do what needs to be done."

I walk over to Krule, who is writhing on the ground, trying to pull the super-Sheelds off his body. I approach slowly, raising the spear over my head. Okay, all I need to do is strike. Then, this will all be over.

Or will it?

I look over at the Emperor who is practically salivating. After I deal with Krule, I'll have to face him.

I close my eyes and raise the spear over my head. I just need to do this before Krule knows what's happening. I just need to murder him in cold blood.

But... I can't.

I lower the spear.

"Do it!" the Emperor yells. "Do it now, you fool! Why are you—"

Suddenly, Krule arches his back and yells "GET! OFF!" And the next thing I know, all of the super-Sheelds are blown off his body with incredible force, disappearing into the distant sky.

"No!" the Emperor yells.

"You thought you could suppress my power!" Krule says, rising to his feet. "But that is impossible! Now I will destroy you both!"

I jump back. I think I've just made a huge mistake.

And now Krule is gonna cream me!

But suddenly, a horrible smell hits my nostrils.

"What is that?" Krule says, scrunching up his face.

"Sorry, tri-eyes," comes a girl's voice. "But as the saying goes, 'whoever smelt it dealt it!'"

Just then, a girl in a black-and-white costume bursts onto the scene. It's Skunk Girl?!?

"You won't be destroying anyone today," comes a boy's voice. "Not with a killer headache like this."

And then a big, gray ball SLAMS into Krule's forehead, knocking him off balance.

Pinball? It's Next Gen! They've come back to save me!

"Say cheese!" comes another girl's voice. But this time I know who it is.

"Selfie!" I yell. "Stay back!"

But as she raises her phone, Krule is ready for her.

His third eye lights up and Selfie's eyes flash green!

No! He's got her! She'll be his slave!

Without a second thought, I lift my spear and throw it at Krule! But unlike my Epic-a-rang disaster, this time the spear sails right over Selfie's head and lands true, plunging deep into Krule's third eye!

"AAAHH!" Krule screams, reaching for the spear as green blood pours out everywhere.

"Selfie!" I yell, running over to her. "Are you okay?"

"I-I think so," she says, bending over, her eyes turning back to blue. "But things got really weird for a minute."

Whew! That was close. But with Krule finally out of the way, the first part of this nightmare should be—

"YOU ELIMINATED MY POWERS. AND NOW I WILL DESTROY YOU!"

—over?

Seriously? I spin around and my knees wobble, because standing before us is Krule! Blood is still gushing from his third eye but it doesn't seem to matter.

What's it gonna take to get rid of this guy?

And that's when I notice something.

He's holding the bloody spear, and it's pointed at me!

I flinch as the villain rears back his massive arm.

But before he throws it—

FAZZZZZAAAMMM!

"NOOOO!" Krule screams, as the shaft of the spear erupts in a field of electricity. Krule's eyes bulge and his limbs jerk uncontrollably. And then his body falls face-first to the ground in a smoldering heap.

Huh? What just happened?

"Do not celebrate, Champion," the Emperor crows, holding an activator in one hand and a gun pointed at me in the other. "You may think I saved your life, but I am only delaying the inevitable. You see, I had hoped to eliminate the both of you in one shot, but once you threw away my spear, I was left with no choice but to kill you one by one. And since Krule was holding the spear, I could not waste the opportunity. But now it is your turn to die."

For a second I'm confused by what he's saying, but then the pieces come together.

That spear he handed me was booby-trapped with electricity, just like the knife he gave Winch! So, if I had stabbed Krule earlier like he wanted, the Emperor would have electrocuted us both at once! But since I threw the spear away, he couldn't do it.

What a slimeball.

"However, I must congratulate you," the Emperor says. "You fought like a true champion, but now you are expendable."

But as the Emperor raises his weapon at my head, I see a golden helmet bobbing its way towards him. It's the behavior modification helmet! But how?

Then, a German Shephard appears, carrying the helmet in its mouth!

Holy Cow! It's Dog-Gone! He's alive!

"What?" the Emperor cries, as Dog-Gone climbs up his back, knocks off his crown, and slams the helmet over his head.

Now's my chance!

The Emperor drops his gun to remove the helmet, and I spring into action, running straight for him. But he's so tall I'm gonna need help.

"Dog-Gone, sit!" I yell.

As my pooch screeches to a halt, I step on his back and leap up towards the Emperor's head. Then, I reach for the helmet and push the green button. I hear a CLICK as I fly past and land hard on the ground.

Ouch! My right shoulder is on fire, but when I look

back up, the Emperor is standing stock still.

I did it!

"Um, what is that thing?" Pinball asks.

"That, my friend, is a Skelton behavior modification device," I say, getting to my feet and walking over to the Emperor.

I don't know if I'll ever get a chance like this again, so I need to pick my words very, very carefully.

"Listen up, Emperor," I say. "I want you to order every last one of your Skelton operatives off of my planet and I never, ever want you to return. In fact, I want you to forget that Earth even exists. If you ever see it on a map, you will ignore it like it was a figment of your imagination. Do you understand?"

"I understand," the Emperor repeats robotically.

Wow, this might actually work!

"And that's not all," I say. "Under your leadership, the Skelton will become a peaceful Empire. You will find a new, abandoned Homeworld and never, ever bother anyone again. Is that clear?"

"Yes," he says. "That is clear."

"Great," I say. "Oh, and one more thing. That helmet you're wearing is your new crown. You should never remove it under any circumstances or let anyone ever touch it. Are those instructions clear?"

"Yes," he says. "They are clear."

"Good," I say. "Now go, and don't ever come back."

Then, the Emperor turns and walks away.

"Um, are you sure we should just let him go like that?" Skunk Girl asks.

"Yep," I say. "Someone needs to lead the Skelton Empire, and it might as well be their behavior-modified Emperor. Besides, after this, I don't think he'll be bothering anyone ever again."

Just then, I feel something wet nuzzle into my palm.

"Dog-Gone!" I throw my arms around him and we tumble to the ground. "I'm so happy you're alive!" I say as tears roll down my cheeks. "I thought I'd lost you forever. You big dummy, don't ever do that to me again."

"You won't believe this," Selfie says. "But he was waiting for us back at the treehouse. It probably took him days to get there, but after the Pentagon disaster, I don't think he knew where else to go. But once we arrived, he led us right back here."

"You're too smart for your own good," I say, squeezing him even tighter.

"Epic Zero!" comes a familiar man's voice.

Dad? And when I look up, I see the whole gang. Mom, Dad, Grace, and all of the Freedom Force! And behind them are Wind Walker and a whole bunch of other heroes, including the Rising Suns!

"You're alive!" I say, throwing myself into Dad's arms, as more tears stream down my cheeks. "I'm so sorry. I never should have contacted you. I really messed up. I—"

"It's okay, son," Dad whispers. "You did great. You

saved us all."

"Even I've got to hand it to you," Grace says, hugging me. "You're really amazing. And this time my fingers aren't crossed."

"Well, this was fun," TechnocRat says. "But it'll be great to go home again. I've got a hankering for some Camembert cheese. In fact, I think I'll even break out the good stuff."

Home? Oh boy.

"Um," I say, trying to smile. "I've got something I need to tell you guys..."

EPILOGUE

I START A NEW CHAPTER

I grab my popcorn and settle into the command chair.

As I look around the Monitor Room, I'm amazed at how TechnocRat nailed every single detail of the original Waystation. He's calling our new headquarters 'the Waystation 2.0' and he's right. Everything feels exactly the same, but with some pretty cool upgrades.

For one, he built himself an even bigger laboratory, with an indestructible vault to house his precious Camembert cheese. There's also a swimming pool, which seemed like a great idea until Dog-Gone decided to test it out. Now we have to keep a gate around it at all times so I don't end up blow-drying wet fur for hours on end.

There's also a bunch of other new goodies, including a break-away satellite pod on the other side of the Hangar allowing for a quick getaway in case we're boarded again.

If I didn't know better, I'd think TechnocRat was trying to tell me something.

Anyway, it feels great to be home again. After all, we had to spend two months living in a cramped apartment while TechnocRat rebuilt the place. Being together was awesome, but sharing one bathroom among seven people, a teenage girl, and an irritable rat is not so much fun. And forget about ever getting a hot shower!

Oh, another major upgrade I forgot to mention is the Meta Monitor—or should I say, the 'Meta Monitor 2.0.' This version not only monitors Earth for Meta signatures but it now also monitors outer space! Of course, it still needs to work out a few kinks, like the time it mistook a meteor shower for an alien invasion, but it's using artificial intelligence to get more accurate every day.

But the best part of the new Waystation is the enhanced Mission Room communications system. Now, with the simple push of a button, we can have direct communication with not only President Kensington but also Paladin Planet and the Ghost Ship!

And by the way, thank goodness we found the real President Kensington. After the whole Pentagon episode, I feared the world would plunge into chaos without its leaders. But then Mom picked up a faint mental cry for help, and we discovered all of the world's leaders trapped inside a reinforced steel room several levels beneath the Capitol building. They were a bit shaken up, but with the help of the other Meta super teams like the Rising Suns and Los Toros, we got them all back to their home countries safe and sound.

Speaking of the Rising Suns, the Psychics like Mom were able to team up to reverse the behavior modification job done to Zen and the others. It wasn't easy, and once she was back to normal, I was amazed that Zen had no recollection of our fight! Sadly, we learned that Tsunami was the one who passed away in the Emperor's lab. He was a brave hero and we're planning to go to his memorial service in a few days.

It was also hard saying goodbye to the Zodiac and the Intergalactic Paladins. It was great seeing Broog and Quovaar again, and they said they'd help keep a closer eye on our solar system—which I thanked them for.

As for the Zodiac, well, they're galactic adventurers at heart so they didn't stick around for long. But with our improved communications system I've been able to keep in touch with all of them, especially Gemini—sometimes well after bedtime.

Of course, I've had to bribe Dog-Gone with a million doggie treats not to tip off Mom or Dad. But that's okay. After all, I'm just happy he's still around.

I look at the Meta Monitor 2.0 but nothing is happening. C'mon, we need some action.

But just as I stuff a handful of popcorn into my mouth, the Meta Monitor 2.0 blares—

"Alert! Alert! Alert! Meta 1 disturbance. Repeat: Meta 1 disturbance. Power signature identified as Erase Face.

Alert! Alert! Alert!"

Erase Face? That's perfect!

I put down my popcorn, send three signals down to Earth, and leap off the command chair. But as soon as I take my first step down the stairs, I hear CRUNCHING behind me.

"Dog-Gone?" I yell over my shoulder. "Were you invisible the whole time? Get out of my popcorn!"

The box tips over and popcorn spills everywhere, but I don't have time to stop. Instead, I race down the stairs and make a mental note. Despite TechnocRat's upgrades, he forgot to install the heat-seeking cameras I asked for.

I bolt through the Galley where I find my parents sitting at the table.

"You taking this one?" Dad asks, sipping his coffee without even looking up from his newspaper.

"Yep, it's a Meta 1," I say, jogging through.

"Have fun," Mom says. "And be back by dinner. It's meatloaf."

"I hate meatloaf!" I say, exiting into the corridor.

I turn a corner and nearly crash into Grace.

"I've got it," I say.

"I figured," she says. "Say hi to your friends for me. And let them know I think they're in good hands. You're a pretty great leader, Elliott."

"Gee," I say, stopping for a second. "Thanks."

"Of course, I might have my toes crossed," Grace says with a wink. "Go get 'em, squirt."

I smile and step into the new Transporter Room. I key in the coordinates and feel the unnerving pins-and-needles sensation of my atoms dissipating. Seconds later, I'm pulled back together at the base of a treehouse.

"It's about time," Pinball says. "We got your signal, like, five minutes ago."

"Sorry," I say, "I got... hung up for a bit."

"Are we ready to go?" Skunk Girl says. "I'm dying to stink something up!"

"Yeah," I say, but then I notice someone is missing. "Where's Selfie?"

"Right here," she says, running over. "Hey."

"Hey," I say, unable to stop my big smile.

"Um, awkward," Pinball says. "Can we go now?"

"What? Oh, right," I say. "Okay team, we're about to do battle with Erase Face. He's a Meta 1 with the ability to wipe things away with his nose. Yes, I know it sounds ridiculous, but don't underestimate him. And please, don't approach him from straight on. Got it?"

"Got it, boss," Skunk Girl says, with a salute.

I look them in the eyes. They're eager to learn and want to do what's right. And for a second, it feels kind of weird that they're hanging on my every word. But then I realize I can really help them, and for the first time, I realize I wouldn't want it any other way.

"Okay, Next Gen," I say. "Get ready, because it's Fight Time!"

They nod, and then we're off!

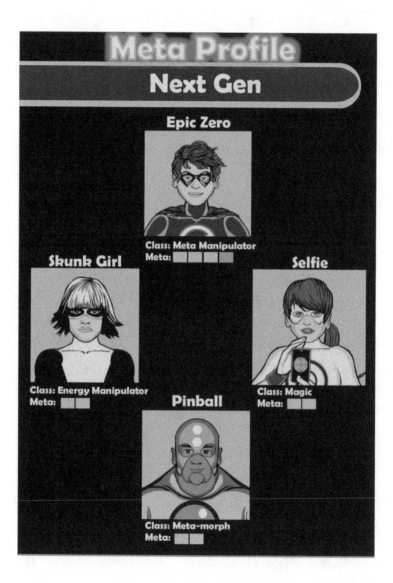

YOU CAN MAKE A BIG DIFFERENCE

Calling all heroes! I need your help to get Epic Zero 6 in front of more readers.

Reviews are extremely helpful in getting attention for my books. I wish I had the marketing muscle of the major publishers, but instead, I have something far more valuable, loyal readers, just like you! Your generosity in providing an honest review will help bring this book to the attention of more readers.

So, if you've enjoyed this book, I would be very grateful if you could spare a minute to leave a review on the book's Amazon page. Thanks for your support!

Stay Epic!

R.L. Ullman

META POWERS GLOSSARY

FROM THE META MONITOR:

There are nine known Meta power classifications. These classifications have been established to simplify Meta identification and provide a quick framework to understand a Meta's potential powers and capabilities. **Note:** Metas can possess powers in more than one classification. In addition, Metas can evolve over time in both the powers they express, as well as the effectiveness of their powers.

Due to the wide range of Meta abilities, superpowers have been further segmented into power levels. Power levels differ across Meta power classifications. In general, the following power levels have been established:

- Meta 0: Displays no Meta power.
- Meta 1: Displays limited Meta power.
- Meta 2: Displays considerable Meta power.
- Meta 3: Displays extreme Meta power.

The following is a brief overview of the nine Meta power classifications.

ENERGY MANIPULATION:

Energy Manipulation is the ability to generate, shape, or act as a conduit, for various forms of energy. Energy Manipulators can control energy by focusing or redirecting energy towards a specific target or shaping/reshaping energy for a specific task. Energy Manipulators are often impervious to the forms of energy they can manipulate.

Examples of the types of energies utilized by Energy Manipulators include, but are not limited to:

- Atomic
- Chemical
- Cosmic
- Electricity
- Gravity
- Heat
- Light
- Magnetic
- Sound
- Space
- Time

Note: the fundamental difference between an Energy Manipulator and a Meta-morph with Energy Manipulation capability is that an Energy Manipulator does not change their physical, molecular state to either generate or transfer energy (see META-MORPH).

FLIGHT:
Flight is the ability to fly, glide, or levitate above the Earth's surface without the use of an external source (e.g. jetpack). Flight can be accomplished through a variety of methods, these include, but are not limited to:

- Reversing the forces of gravity
- Riding air currents
- Using planetary magnetic fields
- Wings

Metas exhibiting Flight can range from barely sustaining flight a few feet off the ground to reaching the far limits of outer space.

Often, Metas with Flight ability also display the complementary ability of Super-Speed. However, it can be difficult to decipher if Super-Speed is a Meta power in its own right or is simply a function of combining the Meta's Flight ability with the Earth's natural gravitational force.

MAGIC:

Magic is the ability to display a wide variety of Meta abilities by channeling the powers of a secondary magical or mystical source. Known secondary sources of Magic powers include, but are not limited to:

- Alien lifeforms
- Dark arts
- Demonic forces
- Departed souls
- Mystical spirits

Typically, the forces of Magic are channeled through an enchanted object. Known magical, enchanted objects include:

- Amulets
- Books
- Cloaks
- Gemstones
- Wands

- Weapons

Some Magicians can transport themselves into the mystical realm of their magical source. They may also have the ability to transport others into and out of these realms as well.

Note: the fundamental difference between a Magician and an Energy Manipulator is that a Magician typically channels their powers from a mystical source that likely requires the use of an enchanted object to express these powers (see ENERGY MANIPULATOR).

META MANIPULATION:

Meta Manipulation is the ability to duplicate or negate the Meta powers of others. Meta Manipulation is a rare Meta power and can be extremely dangerous if the Meta Manipulator is capable of manipulating the powers of multiple Metas at one time. Meta Manipulators who can manipulate the powers of several Metas at once have been observed to reach Meta 4 power levels.

Based on the unique powers of the Meta Manipulator, it is hypothesized that other abilities could include altering or controlling the powers of others. Despite their tremendous abilities, Meta Manipulators are often unable to generate powers of their own and are limited to manipulating the powers of others. When not utilizing their abilities, Meta Manipulators may be vulnerable to attack.

Note: It has been observed that a Meta Manipulator requires close physical proximity to a Meta target to fully manipulate their power. When fighting a Meta

Manipulator, it is advised to stay at a reasonable distance and to attack from long range. Meta Manipulators have been observed manipulating the powers of others up to 100 yards away.

META-MORPH:

Meta-morph is the ability to display a wide variety of Meta abilities by "morphing" all, or part, of one's physical form from one state into another. There are two sub-types of Meta-morphs:

- Physical
- Molecular

Physical morphing occurs when a Meta-morph transforms their physical state to express their powers. Physical Meta-morphs typically maintain their human physiology while exhibiting their powers (with the exception of Shapeshifters). Types of Physical morphing include, but are not limited to:

- Invisibility
- Malleability (elasticity/plasticity)
- Physical by-products (silk, toxins, etc...)
- Shapeshifting
- Size changes (larger or smaller)

Molecular morphing occurs when a Meta-morph transforms their molecular state from a normal physical state to a non-physical state to express their powers. Types of Molecular morphing include, but are not limited to:

- Fire
- Ice
- Rock
- Sand
- Steel
- Water

Note: Because Meta-morphs can display abilities that mimic all other Meta power classifications, it can be difficult to properly identify a Meta-morph upon the first encounter. However, it is critical to carefully observe how their powers manifest, and, if it is through Physical or Molecular morphing, you can be certain you are dealing with a Meta-morph.

PSYCHIC:

Psychic is the ability to use one's mind as a weapon. There are two sub-types of Psychics:

- Telepaths
- Telekinetics

Telepathy is the ability to read and influence the thoughts of others. While Telepaths often do not appear to be physically intimidating, their power to penetrate minds can often result in more devastating damage than a physical assault.

Telekinesis is the ability to manipulate physical objects with one's mind. Telekinetics can often move objects with their mind that are much heavier than they could move physically. Many Telekinetics can also make objects move at very high speeds.

Note: Psychics are known to strike from long distance, and, in a fight, it is advised to incapacitate them as quickly as possible. Psychics often become physically drained from the extended use of their powers.

SUPER-INTELLIGENCE:

Super-Intelligence is the ability to display levels of intelligence above standard genius intellect. Super-Intelligence can manifest in many forms, including, but not limited to:

- Superior analytical ability
- Superior information synthesizing
- Superior learning capacity
- Superior reasoning skills

Note: Super-Intellects continuously push the envelope in the fields of technology, engineering, and weapons development. Super-Intellects are known to invent new approaches to accomplish previously impossible tasks. When dealing with a Super-Intellect, you should be mentally prepared to face challenges that have never been encountered before. In addition, Super-Intellects can come in all shapes and sizes. The most advanced Super-Intellects have originated from non-human creatures.

SUPER-SPEED:

Super-Speed is the ability to display movement at remarkable physical speeds above standard levels of speed. Metas with Super-Speed often exhibit complementary abilities to movement that include, but are not limited to:

- Enhanced endurance
- Phasing through solid objects
- Super-fast reflexes
- Time travel

Note: Metas with Super-Speed often have an equally super metabolism, burning thousands of calories per minute, and requiring them to eat many extra meals a day to maintain consistent energy levels. It has been observed that Metas exhibiting Super-Speed are quick thinkers, making it difficult to keep up with their thought process.

SUPER-STRENGTH:
Super-Strength is the ability to utilize muscles to display remarkable levels of physical strength above expected levels of strength. Metas with Super-Strength can lift or push objects that are well beyond the capability of an average member of their species. Metas exhibiting Super-Strength can range from lifting objects twice their weight to incalculable levels of strength allowing for the movement of planets.

Metas with Super-Strength often exhibit complementary abilities to strength that include, but are not limited to:

- Earthquake generation through stomping
- Enhanced jumping
- Invulnerability
- Shockwave generation through clapping

Note: Metas with Super-Strength may not always possess this strength evenly. Metas with Super-Strength have been observed to demonstrate powers in only one arm or leg.

META PROFILE CHARACTERISTICS

FROM THE META MONITOR:

In addition to having a strong working knowledge of a Meta's powers and capabilities, it is also imperative to understand the key characteristics that form the core of their character. When facing or teaming up with Metas, understanding their key characteristics will help you gain deeper insight into their mentality and strategic potential.

What follows is a brief explanation of the five key characteristics you should become familiar with. **Note**: the data that appears in each Meta profile has been compiled from live field activity.

COMBAT:

The ability to defeat a foe in hand-to-hand combat.

DURABILITY:

The ability to withstand significant wear, pressure, or damage.

LEADERSHIP:

The ability to lead a team of disparate personalities and powers to victory.

STRATEGY:

The ability to find, and successfully exploit, a foe's weakness.

WILLPOWER:

The ability to persevere, despite seemingly insurmountable odds.

GET MORE EPIC!

Don't miss any of the Epic action!

Get a **FREE** copy of
Epic Zero Extra: Tales of a Superhero Screw Up
only at rlullman.com.

ABOUT THE AUTHOR

R.L. Ullman is the bestselling author of the award-winning EPIC ZERO series and the award-winning MONSTER PROBLEMS series. He creates fun, engaging page-turners that captivate the imaginations of kids and adults alike. His original, relatable characters face adventure and adversity that bring out their inner strengths. He's frequently distracted thinking up new stories, and once got lost in his own neighborhood. You can learn more about what R.L. is up to at rlullman.com, and if you see him wandering around your street please point him in the right direction home.

For news, updates, and free stuff, please sign up for the Epic Newsflash at rlullman.com.

ACKNOWLEDGMENTS

Without the support of these brave heroes, I would have been trampled by supervillains before I could bring this series to print. I would like to thank my wife, Lynn (a.k.a. Mrs. Marvelous); my daughter Olivia (a.k.a. Ms. Positivity); and my son Matthew (a.k.a. Captain Creativity). I would also like to thank all of the readers out there who have connected with Elliott and his amazing family. Stay Epic!